"I would like—" the duke's voice was low and husky now, and every word he spoke sent a shiver through Anna **"—to do so many things with you. I know that we've only just met, but I feel..."**

James paused and then continued, "I'm sorry. That's far too much. To begin with." He tugged her hair very slightly, very gently, so that her head was angled exactly beneath his. And then, very, very slowly, he leaned toward her and brushed her lips with his. "I would very much like to call on you tomorrow."

"I would like that, too, but..." Anna barely knew what she was saying. She was very aware that she had to tell him something *now* so that he wouldn't be holding any misconceptions, but she was even more aware of how he was holding her and where his lips had just touched hers.

Author Note

I hope you enjoy reading *When Cinderella Met the Duke* as much as I enjoyed writing it!

I wanted to write a Cinderella-themed story, but with a bit of a twist.

James, our hero, needs to get married to produce an heir, but—scarred by bereavement—does not want to fall in love. But then he meets Anna at a ball and finds himself smitten at first sight... Only for her to run away at midnight, and for him then to discover that she is not who he thought she was. I loved exploring his internal conflict as his love for Anna grew.

In Anna, I wanted to write a heroine for the ages, a strong woman with a determination to make her own way within the constraints of the era she lives in. Offered the opportunity by her godmother to become her (actually quite unnecessary) companion, she turns it down and takes up a post as a governess to earn her living. Anna's life history has taught her not to trust men, specifically their loyalty, and I very much enjoyed following her path to finding the courage to allow herself to fall in love with James and marry him.

I also of course enjoyed, as always, the gorgeous Regency London setting—and researching all the different ice cream flavors available then... I'm quite tempted by artichoke and Parmesan!

Thank you so much for reading!

WHEN CINDERELLA MET THE DUKE

SOPHIA WILLIAMS

HISTORICAL

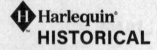

Harlequin® HISTORICAL

ISBN-13: 978-1-335-53991-5

Recycling programs for this product may not exist in your area.

When Cinderella Met the Duke

Copyright © 2024 by Jo Lovett-Turner

 Harlequin Enterprises ULC
22 Adelaide St. West, 41st Floor
Toronto, Ontario M5H 4E3, Canada
www.Harlequin.com

Printed in U.S.A.

Sophia Williams lives in London with her family. She has loved reading Regency romances for as long as she can remember and is delighted now to be writing them for Harlequin. When she isn't chasing her children around or writing (or pretending to write but actually googling for hero inspiration and pictures of gorgeous Regency dresses), she enjoys reading, tennis and wine.

Books by Sophia Williams

Harlequin Historical

How the Duke Met His Match
The Secret She Kept from the Earl

Look out for more books from Sophia Williams coming soon.

Visit the Author Profile page
at Harlequin.com.

To William

Chapter One

Miss Anna Blake

London,
November 1817

'I am really not certain that this is a good idea,' Miss Anna Blake said, surveying herself in the looking glass in front of her. She *wanted* it to be a good idea, because she didn't know whether she'd ever again have the opportunity to wear a dress as wonderful as this or be able to go to another Society ball, but…

'Nonsense. You deserve to have one last evening of enjoyment.' Anna's godmother, Lady Derwent, tweaked the gauze overdress of Anna's ball gown into place and gave the tiniest of ladylike sniffs before wiping very delicately under her eyes with her beringed fingers. 'I declare, you look like something out of a fairy tale, my dear: so beautiful. Your mother would have been so proud.'

'Thank you, but…' Anna began again. She was quite

sure that her mother would *not* have recommended quite such an audacious deception. She had practised a deception of her own, when she'd eloped with Anna's father, and had then had to spend Anna's entire childhood attempting—with little success—to repair the damage done by the elopement. She had therefore been particularly desirous of Anna's living as respectably as possible. The plan for this evening was *not* respectable.

'You're being far too cautious,' Anna's best friend, Lady Maria Swanley, told her. 'If anyone should ever find out—which they won't—it will be *I* whom they accuse of wrongdoing.'

'Hmm,' said Anna.

Nearly ten years of close friendship with Lady Maria, since they had entered Bath's strictest seminary together, had taught her that Maria's plots gave rise to much enjoyment but usually ended badly, for Anna, at least.

As the daughter of a rich earl, Lady Maria was usually protected from reprimand. Anna, by contrast, was the daughter of a groom. She was also the granddaughter of an earl, and sponsored by Lady Derwent, one of Society's most redoubtable matrons and a great friend of her late mother's, but in the eyes of Miss Courthope, the seminary headmistress, she was her father's daughter and someone who could be punished much more thoroughly than could Maria, so whenever Anna had engaged in any mischief—usually with Maria—she had afterwards felt the full force of Miss Courthope's ire.

That was one thing, and Anna had considered Miss Courthope's punishments a small price to pay for how much she'd enjoyed misbehaving, but hoodwinking most of the *ton* was another. Surely that could give rise to any number of consequences considerably greater than having to write out one's catechism three times or pen a letter of apology to the dance master.

'What if Lady Puntney finds out? What if I oversleep tomorrow?' Anna was starting work as a governess for the Puntney family in the morning. 'And what if your parents find out?' *How* had she allowed herself to be talked into this? Well, she knew how: both Lady Maria and Lady Derwent could be extremely persuasive and, if she was honest, Anna had been very happy to allow herself to be persuaded, and it was only now that the deception was almost under way that she was beginning to acknowledge her doubts.

'If my parents find out, it is likely that they will also have found out about my engagement to my darling Clarence, and they will be interested only in that,' Maria said.

Anna nodded; that much was true. Lady Maria's beloved Clarence was a curate of very uncertain means, and her parents had their sights set on the Duke of Amscott, no less, as their only daughter's future husband.

Anna was not convinced that her friend was making a sensible choice; Clarence might seem perfect now to Maria, but what if things became difficult in due course? He was of course a man of the cloth, so would—one would hope—hold himself to higher standards than did other men, but if he was anything like Anna's father and grandfather, his love would not endure in the face of life's obstacles.

When Anna's mother had fallen in love at the age of eighteen with one of her father's grooms, and then become with child and eloped with him, her father—

Anna's grandfather—had disowned her and refused ever to see her again. He had died a few years later. And after the money raised from the sale of Anna's mother's jewels ran out, Anna's father had left to make a new life for himself in America, with no apparent further thought for his wife and daughter. When Anna had lost her mother, she had written to her father, and had received his— very short and not particularly heartfelt—reply over six months later. She knew that he had written it himself— her mother had taught him to read and write in the early days of their marriage and she recognised his handwriting—so had to assume that it did express his own sentiments. He had not suggested that she join him in Canada or that he attempt to support her in any way whatsoever.

Anna had been rescued from penury by the women in her life—her mother's maid and then Lady Derwent— and she did not believe that men were to be relied upon. Lady Derwent had confirmed this belief; she had told Anna on more than one occasion that she was *extremely* happy to be a widow.

'And in the meantime,' Maria interrupted her thoughts, 'I *cannot* go to the ball.'

The Dowager Duchess of Amscott was holding the first grand ball of the Season this evening, and, according to Lady Derwent, everyone expected the duke to be there, searching for a wife. Lady Maria's birth, beauty and large dowry made her an obvious candidate for the position. When her parents had been called away and she had been entrusted to Lady Derwent to chaperone her this evening, Maria had suggested, most persuasively, as was her wont, that Anna attend in her place.

She had waxed lyrical about the dress that Anna

would wear, the people she would see, the dancing, the food, the enjoyment of participating in such an excellent but entirely harmless deception. Lady Derwent had immediately echoed her suggestions, and Anna had found herself agreeing most thoroughly with everything they said. Now, though…

'Lady Puntney will not find out,' Lady Derwent stated, with great certainty. 'Dressed as you are now, you look like one of Shakespeare's fairy queens. Lord Byron himself would write quite lyrically about you, I'm sure. When attired in the *garments*—' she scrunched her face disapprovingly '—you will wear as governess, you will still look beautiful, of course, but you will look quite different. I do not believe that anyone will make the connection. And we will leave at midnight so that you will not be too tired on the morrow.'

'The timing is quite serendipitous,' Maria mused. 'Had this ball not been my first, had I not been incarcerated in the country in mourning for so many years so that I know no one in London—' Maria's family had suffered a series of bereavements '—and had my parents not been forced to leave town and entrust me to the care of dear Lady Derwent—' Lady Maria's grandmother was ill and her mother had left post-haste, accompanied by her husband, to visit her in her hour of need '—this would not have been possible. And by the time my parents return, Clarence and I shall be formally affianced, and no one will make me attend any more balls as a rich-husband-seeking young lady. So it will all be perfect.'

She smiled at Anna.

'You look beautiful. That dress becomes you wonderfully. Perhaps you will find a beau of your own this evening, and marry rather than take up your position.'

Anna rolled her eyes at her friend. 'I shall be very happy as a governess.' She wasn't *entirely* convinced that that was true, but it would be better than relying on a man to protect her, only to be abandoned when he lost interest in her; and she was certainly very lucky to have obtained her position with the Puntneys.

'Harumph.' Lady Derwent did not approve of Anna's desire to be independent; she had asked her more than once to live with her as a companion, despite her obvious lack of need for one. 'Let us go. You will not wish to miss any part of the ball, Anna.'

'What if you change your mind in future, Maria?' Anna worried. 'How will you take your place in Society after I have attended this ball as you?'

'No one would ever dare to question me,' Lady Derwent said. 'Should you in the future change your mind, Maria, and decide that you do not after all wish to marry an impecunious curate with few prospects, and that you wish to take your place at balls as yourself, I shall inform anyone who questions me that their eyesight is perhaps failing them and that the Lady Maria they met at the Amscott ball was of course you, and no one will contradict me.'

Certainly, very few people, including Anna, chose to disagree very often with Lady Derwent.

Anna turned to look again at her image in the glass. She *loved* this dress. It would be such a shame not to show it off at the ball. She *loved* parties—the small number that she had been to. She *loved* dancing. And everyone who was anyone amongst London's glittering *haut ton* would be there, and she would *love* to see them all, and witness and take part in such an event.

She straightened her shoulders and beamed at the reflection of her two companions before turning back round.

'You are both right,' she said. She was going to take this wonderful opportunity and enjoy it to the full before starting her new, possibly quite dull life on the morrow.

'It will be so diverting to know that you are practising such a masquerade,' Maria said. 'A huge secret that no one else knows. And you will enjoy the dancing very much, I am sure.'

'Thank you, Maria,' Anna said.

'No, no.' Maria hugged her. '*I* must thank *you*. Just make sure you enjoy yourself.'

'I just want to check one final time that you are absolutely certain?' Anna asked again.

'We are certain.' Lady Derwent was already standing and moving towards the door. 'Nothing can possibly go wrong.'

Chapter Two

James, Duke of Amscott

'And that is all for now,' concluded the Dowager Duchess of Amscott, as she folded into neat squares the piece of paper upon which she had scribed her list of possible candidates for the hand of her son, James, Duke of Amscott, before leaving her escritoire to join him on the sofa opposite.

James raised an eyebrow. 'Are you intending to share the contents of your list with me?'

'Maybe. Maybe not.' She waved the piece of paper under his nose before whisking it away and tucking it into her reticule.

James laughed. The idea of getting married was not at all funny, but his mother could nearly always raise a smile from him. Which was impressive, given all that she had gone through in recent years, with the death first of her husband and then of James's two older brothers.

'On a serious note,' his mother said, 'I will of course discuss the list with you, but I feel that it might be best for you first to meet the various young ladies without any preconceptions. You are fortunate in having no need to marry for money and being able therefore to choose any young lady—of good birth, of course—for love.'

James looked down at his knees for a moment, to hide his eyes from her as a chill ran over him.

He did not want to marry for love.

He did not wish to love someone so deeply that he would be broken if anything happened to her, as his mother had been at the loss of her husband and two oldest sons, and as he and his sisters had also been.

Also, and even more importantly, he did not wish someone to love *him* deeply, because he wouldn't wish anyone else to be devastated if he died, and he veered between terror and resignation at the thought that it seemed extremely likely that he would die young; the doctors were not sure what had caused the early deaths of his father and brothers but their symptoms had all been similar, and it did not seem unlikely that their illnesses had been due to a family trait. It would be bad enough thinking of the pain that would cause his mother and sisters, but for him to choose to marry someone who loved him deeply only for the pain of loss to be inflicted on her too would be awful.

'James?'

'Yes, Mama. What an...excellent plan.' He could not tell her how he felt; he could not add to her sadness, especially when she was doing so well herself at pretending to be happy. He must maintain his own stiff upper lip, as she did.

And his emotions were confused. Because he *needed* to produce an heir. His current heir was a distant cousin residing in Canada, and James had no way of knowing whether the man would—in the event of James's death—look after James's mother and younger sisters in the way that he would wish. It would be infinitely preferable for a son of James's—infant or adult—to become the new duke.

And the existence of an heir—his son—would of course lessen his family's grief on James's death, in addition to securing their future. His wife would have a child or children to love, and his mother had already proved herself to be a most doting grandmother to his oldest sister's two young daughters.

He raised his eyes to his mother's and smiled as sincerely as he could.

'That is settled then.' She rose from the sofa. 'You will meet as many ladies as possible this evening, and should you develop a preference, you may undertake to improve your acquaintance of the young lady in question. If you do not have a preference, we will revert to my list.'

James rose too. 'Excellent.' *God.*

'We must hasten. The first of our guests will arrive soon.' She held her arm out imperiously.

They were hosting the first big ball of this year's London Season, and James's mother believed that the whole of Society would be scrabbling to attend. She was almost certainly right: wealthy dukes were always popular, irrespective of their personal attributes. They were even more popular when they were nearing thirty and unmarried.

He laughed at his mother's haughty gesture, and took her arm, wondering as he did so what chance there was that he would meet someone this evening with whom

he could fall in love, should he allow himself to do so—
he would not—or whether he would be happy to marry
someone from the list.

He did need to marry.

And while he did not desire a love match, he did wish
to choose his own bride rather than have one foisted
upon him by his mother. He would like someone whose
conversation he enjoyed, for example, although he probably wouldn't choose to live permanently with anyone
quite as opinionated as his mother and sisters were…

As they entered the ballroom, his mother's voice
pierced his thoughts. 'Amscott. I was telling you about
my decorations.' She hadn't allowed him to see the
themed room until now, eager, she said, to spring a surprise on him—or perhaps just to avert the strong possibility of his cavilling at her evident extraordinarily high
expenditure. He had in fact been happy to indulge her,
delighted to see her take an interest in something again;
she had struggled with listlessness in the aftermath of
their bereavements.

'I beg your pardon, Mama. I was lost in admiration
of your design of the room.' It was certainly remarkable—and must indeed have cost a small fortune. The
ballroom of Amscott House had been transformed into
an exotic fruit orchard. There were so many orange and
lemon trees—surely more than in the glasshouses of the
rest of England combined—that the room had a definite
citrusy scent. And were those…pineapple trees?

'I wished to make a splash, and I believe we shall do
so. In addition, our ball will *smell* nicer than everyone
else's.' His mother's air of complacence made him laugh

again. 'So many hot bodies in the same room can often be quite unbearable.'

'Impressive forethought.'

'I must confess that I did not realise how very much scent the trees would give off,' his mother confided, 'but I am quite delighted now at how I shall be setting both a visual design *and* an olfactory trend.'

The first guests were announced before they had the opportunity to engage in further conversation, and James became fully occupied in greeting dandified men, bejewelled matrons, their eager-to-please debutante charges and the occasional actual friend of his.

'Lady Derwent and Lady Maria Swanley,' a footman announced, as a tall woman, her air almost as imperious as that of James's mother, swept into the room with a smaller and younger lady, who was dressed in a silvery, sparkly dress.

'Good evening.' Lady Derwent curtsied the tiniest amount in James's mother's direction, her demeanour as though she was conferring an enormous favour on the duchess, who responded with the smallest of smiles. James made a mental note to ask his mother on the morrow what argument she and Lady Derwent held; there was clearly some animosity between the two women, and his mother's stories were always amusing. 'Lady Maria is under my charge this evening; dear Lady Swanley has been called to Viscountess Massey's sickbed.'

'I am so sorry to hear that your grandmother is ill,' James's mother told Lady Maria.

'Thank you; we hope very much that she will make a full and speedy recovery.' Lady Maria's voice was musical, clear and warm in tone, so lovely to listen to that James instinctively looked more closely in her direction.

Her hair was a light brown, thick and glossy, her eyes green, her skin clear and her features regular, and her dress—cut low at the bosom and high at the waist—became her very well. She was certainly attractive, but, when his thoughts wandered vaguely to whether she would be on his mother's marriage candidate list, he decided that it was irrelevant; she was probably a very pleasant lady, but there were any number of pleasant, attractive young ladies here, and he could think of no reason that he would choose this lady over any other.

Indeed, how *would* he choose a bride given that his choice would not be directed by his falling in love? Perhaps he should ask his oldest two sisters which young ladies they got on with best.

'My son, the Duke of Amscott,' James's mother said, and Lady Maria turned in his direction with a smile.

And, good Lord, the smile was extraordinary. It displayed perfect, even teeth, it was wide, it was infectious, it showed one delightful dimple just to the left of her mouth, it was *beautiful*. James felt it through his entire body, almost uncomfortably so.

'Delighted to meet you.' His own mouth was broadening into a wide smile in response to Lady Maria's, almost of its own volition.

Lady Maria curtseyed and held out two fingers, smiling now as though she was almost on the brink of laughter, her eyes dancing. James had no idea what she was finding quite so funny, but he knew that he wanted to find out. He had the strangest feeling, in fact, that he wanted to find out everything about her, which was a

ridiculous sensation to have, given that the entire sum
of knowledge he had about her was that she was a small,
pleasant-looking woman with a musical voice and the
most beguiling smile and was accompanied by Lady
Derwent.

He leaned forward a little and spoke into her ear, just
for her, comfortable in the knowledge that the hubbub
of voices around them would make it very difficult for
anyone else to hear.

'Do you have a joke that you wish to share?' He accompanied his words with a smile, to ensure that Lady
Maria would know that he was funning rather than reprimanding her in any way. He would not normally speak
to a stranger, a debutante, in such a manner, but then
debutantes did not usually look as though they held a
big and amusing secret. And he couldn't remember the
last time—if ever—that he'd had such a strong sense
that he *would* get to know a particular person very well.

'No, Your Grace.' Her smile was no less mirthful than
before as she continued, 'I am perhaps just overwhelmed
by the occasion.' Her words did not ring true; she did
not seem in the slightest bit overwhelmed.

She looked around the room before returning her regard to his. 'I adore these plants. They are quite remarkable. I have never seen a lemon or orange tree outside
the covers of a book.'

'Remarkable indeed,' James agreed. 'I have it on the
highest authority that the scent as well as the décor will
make this one of the most successful balls of the Season.'

'I think your authority is right,' Lady Maria said very
gravely. 'Every ball is judged by its scent. And it is particularly clever to use trees that will, I presume, no lon-

ger be bearing fruit as we enter the winter, so that no other host will be able to replicate this.'

'I had not thought of that. The design is my mother's; you and she are obviously both more astute than I.'

'Thank you; I am of course regularly complimented on my ballroom scent knowledge.'

She twinkled up at him as she spoke, and James laughed.

And then he found himself saying, 'May I have the pleasure of taking the first dance with you?'

As he finished the question, he realised the import of his words: asking a young lady whom he had never previously met, and who was presumably at her first ball, for the first dance could be taken as a mark of quite particular regard. Certainly, if he did not then wish to further their acquaintance, he would have to navigate things very carefully: on the one hand, he would have to ensure on his own account that he did not appear to single her out for any other special attention; but he would also, for her sake, have to make sure that he did not appear to slight her.

Somehow, though, he didn't mind; he again had the strangest sensation that he *had* to get to know Lady Maria better.

'I'm sure Lady Maria would be delighted.' Lady Derwent had clearly overheard his words and, as any good chaperone ought to do when a wealthy unmarried duke asked her charge to dance, was doing her best to ensure that his request was granted. In fact, if he wasn't mistaken, she had just given Lady Maria a small but quite forceful nudge.

To James's admiration, Lady Maria didn't acknowledge the nudge at all, not even glancing in Lady Derwent's direction before saying, 'I would indeed be delighted.'

'Amscott.' His mother's tone was sharp; she had clearly overheard his question and was less happy about it than Lady Derwent had been. 'You will remember my dear friend Countess Montague and her daughter Lady Helena Montague.'

As the introductions continued, James found his gaze following Lady Maria until she was swallowed up by the hordes of people swirling around her. Once he'd lost sight of her, he couldn't find her again, however hard he tried. And, he realised a few minutes later, when his mother remarked acerbically on yet another lapse in his attention, he was trying very hard to see her.

It would have been easier had she been less diminutive in stature, of course.

James had hitherto always thought he was more attracted to taller ladies, but he now realised that he'd been quite wrong.

Good God. At the age of twenty-nine years old, he was behaving like an infatuated moonling in his first Season. One beautiful smile had turned his mind.

He couldn't even remember what he'd been thinking about women and marriage only an hour ago. He was certain that he hadn't wanted to find any woman this attractive, but he wasn't quite sure why. Attraction and love were not the same thing, after all.

'Amscott.' His mother's sharpness had reached the pitch where it could cut a steak; he should concentrate harder on these introductions. She was a devoted mother and a generous-spirited woman, but she did not appreciate inattention.

* * *

Eventually, the introductions were completed and it was time for the first dance.

As he made his way across the room to where Lady Maria was standing with Lady Derwent, James was conscious of a genuine increase in his heart rate, which had him almost physically shaking his head at himself. After all, he didn't even know now whether he'd been imagining how attractive he'd found Lady Maria; perhaps when he saw her again he'd realise that he'd been quite mistaken.

And then, over other people's heads, he did catch sight of her. She was standing with some other debutantes, laughing at something another young lady had just said. Lady Maria then said something in her turn, and the whole little group joined in with the laughter—full, shoulder-shaking laughter, not just polite Society titters. He couldn't help smiling just watching them and realised that he would very much like to know what the joke was. And when he saw Lady Maria beam at the other ladies, he knew that he had not been mistaken in the slightest; she was remarkably attractive.

Perhaps half a minute later, he was standing in front of Lady Maria and Lady Derwent, with his heels snapped together, bowing his head to both ladies.

Lady Derwent was, unsurprisingly, wreathed in smiles. James didn't flatter himself that he personally was a hugely attractive catch on the marriage mart; that would presumably depend on a lady's particular taste. He did, though, believe that an unmarried duke in possession of a good fortune must always be attractive to the vast majority of young ladies and their chaperones, and it appeared that Lady Derwent was no exception.

Lady Maria was also smiling, but not quite so widely as when they'd met or when she'd been laughing with the other young ladies. He hoped she wasn't regretting agreeing to this dance. Perhaps she was one of those rare debutantes who had no wish to marry a duke.

Good God. In the past few minutes he must have thought about marriage at least five times. It was as though he had, like many men before him, lost his head to one pretty face. And good God again, he felt as though he didn't care and indeed would be more than happy to follow his instincts and court the young lady most assiduously.

As Lady Maria placed her fingertips lightly on his arm, he knew that he had to be imagining it, but it was as though this moment of their first touch was extremely significant, as though the contact was branding him in some way; he had the strangest sense that it would be the first of many such touches. Extraordinary; he was never this fanciful.

'You are recently arrived in London, I understand?' he asked her as they wove through the crowds of guests towards the dance floor.

'Yes,' she confirmed. 'I was previously in the country. I very much like London and over the past week or two have enjoyed prevailing upon my godmother to show me any number of places that I believe interested me a good deal more than they interested her.'

James laughed and then queried, 'You have been spending time with your godmother?'

'Yes. I… Yes, Lady Derwent, I mean. My mother was called away some time ago to be with my grandmother.'

'Oh, I see. I had understood your mother to have left town very recently.'

'I… No. Not particularly recently. Less recently than you might think. Do you reside in London all year round, Your Grace?'

Bizarrely, given that they really did not know each other, *Your Grace* sounded far too formal on Lady Maria's lips.

Suppressing a desire to ask her to call him James, and wishing that he could call her a simple Maria, he said, 'I have only recently inherited the dukedom. I imagine that I will spend the Season in London and the remainder of the year in the country.' He had the most insane urge to tell her that he was really quite flexible and, if his soon-to-be—he hoped—wife wished to spend all her time in London or all her time in the country, he would be quite amenable to either, as long as he could be at her side. He really did seem to have run quite mad. He didn't know Lady Maria. He didn't even know…well, anything at all about her.

And he did *not* wish to marry for love. Did he? No, he did not. *This* was clearly not love. He just had a very strong sense that she would be an excellent life companion, that was all.

He opened his mouth to ask any one of the many thousands of questions to which he'd like to have the answers—such as *Where would you like to live? How old are you?* and, quite possibly, *Would you like to marry me?*—just as she said, 'I'm so sorry to hear that. There can never be a good reason to inherit something.'

'No,' James agreed. 'My brother's death came as a devastating shock to all of us, but especially of course to my mother.' Good God. He never spoke about this, and here he was confiding in a complete stranger. Before he knew anything about her. Truly, something very odd had happened to him.

'I'm so deeply sorry. I can empathise. We have also suffered bereavement in my family. Like most families, I suppose.' Lady Maria paused and then, as though consciously changing the subject, looked around and said, 'I am enjoying this ball enormously.'

James smiled, grateful that she'd lightened the moment. 'So am I. I presume that this is your first?' He was clearly extraordinarily lucky to have met her immediately on her coming out. He was surprised though, now he thought about it: she looked a little older than he would have expected a debutante to be. In the most delightful way. On reflection, he would prefer his wife to be a little older than the youngest of debutantes. That way, their companionship, friendship—certainly not love—would be more balanced.

'Yes. I…' There was that hesitation again. Why did she seem to be choosing her words carefully? Did she have something to hide or was she just nervous at her first ball? He had so many questions about her; he *needed* to get to know her better. 'We were in mourning for a long period, which is why I haven't made my come-out until now.' Oh; perhaps the subject matter would explain her hesitation.

'Of course. I'm sorry.' He wanted to ask whom it was they had been mourning but didn't wish to upset her.

Neither of them had the opportunity to say any more

for the time being. The band had struck up and all involved in the first dance—a quadrille—were taking their places.

'I must apologise,' Lady Maria told him as they came together at the beginning of the dance. 'It is some time since I danced, and I might have forgotten some of the steps.'

'You look remarkably proficient to me,' James told her, wishing very much that this was a waltz so that he might stand close to Lady Maria and talk to her for the duration of the dance. 'It is I who must apologise in advance; there is every possibility that I will tread on your toes.'

Lady Maria shook her head. 'I am not exaggerating when I say that I will be forced to count my steps or I risk causing the entire ensemble to fail. Look.' And she began to mouth numbers, all the while looking straight ahead and smiling serenely, her eyes dancing.

James choked back laughter as they came together and then drew apart, before Lady Maria moved round gracefully, throwing a final 'one and two' at him over her shoulder as he went. James didn't know what Lady Derwent would say if she could hear her charge now, but he was sure that his mother would disapprove; she was a stickler for only the most proper of behaviour in public. James, by contrast, he now realised, had been waiting all his life for a lady who laughed irreverently through her first formal dance.

The nice thing about their dancing a quadrille was that he was able to give full attention to the other ladies he crossed briefly while having ample opportunity to observe Lady Maria's very much in-time and particularly graceful dancing.

She was, he could see, perfectly polite to the other gentlemen she encountered as they all moved around, but perhaps, he fancied—hoped—not quite so sparkling as she had been when talking to him.

Every so often, when he was glancing in her direction, she would look over at him too, and their eyes would catch. James couldn't remember a time when he had felt a greater sense of anticipation and enjoyment of the moments in a set when he would come together with his original partner.

When the dance finished, James said with great reluctance, 'I must escort you back to Lady Derwent.'

'Oh, thank you, but I am taken for the second dance.'

'Oh, yes, I should have assumed that you would be.' He should *not* be feeling mildly—strongly—irritated at the thought of someone else wishing to dance with her. He himself, after all, was about to dance with a different lady. And he barely knew Lady Maria.

'You should indeed have done; once it becomes known that the Duke of Amscott wishes to dance the opening dance with one, one becomes extremely popular with other young men.'

'I am certain that it is you with whom they wish to dance, and not just my partner.' James was quite sure that it wasn't just the social cachet of dancing with him that had attracted others; all she had to do was smile and surely she would have the world at her feet.

Lady Maria smiled at him. He *loved* her smile. 'It is very kind of you to say so.'

He returned the smile and then said, because he

couldn't help it, 'May I have the pleasure of dancing the waltz with you later?'

'I do have one dance left on my card,' she said, 'and I believe that it is a waltz,' and there was that dimple again.

Dancing twice with a lady at a ball was tantamount to stating a very serious intention towards her, especially when that ball was your own. James wondered very briefly what his mother and indeed the whole of the rest of the *ton* would think about the fact that he was making a statement of this magnitude at this very first ball of the Season. And then he realised that he did not care in the slightest. All he cared about, it seemed, was getting to know Lady Maria better.

'And perhaps I might take you into supper?' he suggested.

'That would be delightful,' she said, bestowing yet another stunning smile on him before being whisked away by a far-too-eager—in James's eyes—young viscount.

If his dance with Lady Maria had fairly flown by, the remainder of the dances until supper passed very slowly, other than when he was briefly partnered with Lady Maria during the movements within sets.

Each time that that happened, he felt the most ridiculous lifting of his heart. Truly, he didn't think he'd ever experienced such infatuation in his entire life. Every snatched touch of the hand, smile and couple of words exchanged felt like a gift from heaven. And every time they had to move on from each other, it felt as though he'd been deprived very suddenly.

* * *

Finally, supper was called.

James, wondering at himself, had been, as though under some kind of spell, waiting with increasing impatience for the end of the last set, knowing that supper would be coming. He'd also been unable to prevent himself through the entirety of the dance from keeping a close eye on Lady Maria's whereabouts. Truly, he was behaving like a love-struck youth.

He handed the young lady whom he had just partnered back to her mother and thanked her profusely for the dance, escaped before her mother could hint too forcefully that he might escort her into supper, and made his way over to where he'd last spied Lady Maria.

By the time he got to her, she was surrounded by several young sprigs together with several more mature gentlemen, two of whom were good friends of James's.

'Lady Maria.' James inserted himself between two of the men as he spoke.

'Your Grace.' She smiled at him and he realised that it had to have been at least half an hour since he'd last received a smile from her. He was already basking in the warmth of this latest one; each one felt as though it was a special gift just for him.

He held his arm out to her, internally raising his eyebrows at himself at the way in which his thoughts had suddenly become so poetic.

'Thank you.' She accepted the arm—and good God, he almost shivered at her touch—and smiled around the group of men, and then they began to process with all the other guests towards the supper room.

'I am looking forward to seeing how my mother will

have had the supper room decorated,' he told Lady Maria as they walked. 'I have not yet seen it; I don't know whether she will have continued her theme in there.'

Well. It was fortunate that he was a duke; if this was all the conversation he could provide, he would have to hope that his title would attract Lady Maria.

'I'm sure it will be as striking and beautiful as the ballroom. I look forward to finding out whether it smells as wonderful.'

James was spared from having to search for any more words—truly this was the first time in his life that he'd ever been struck so near dumb—by their entry into the supper room.

And... Good Lord. His mother had certainly not held back.

James and Lady Maria both stood for a moment, staring.

It was Lady Maria who regained her powers of speech first. 'It's...most striking,' she said. 'And elegant.'

James nodded, still speechless. He wasn't sure that *elegant* was the right word for it.

'I like the green,' Lady Maria persisted. 'It's very... botanical. Like the ballroom.'

'It certainly is...apple-coloured,' James said.

'And the pink is quite like a fuchsia. Which is also botanical.'

'Indeed.'

The supper room was hung with lengths of bright pink-and-green-striped silk, and the colour theme continued to the tables, the plates, the *floor*. It was truly the stuff of intense migraines.

In addition, the stripes were so wide but so ubiquitous that certain people's clothing was almost camouflaged.

'I like it.' Lady Maria had clearly entirely recovered from the shock now, and spoke quite definitively. 'I foresee that this will set a fashion for stripes.'

'I sincerely hope that you are wrong. May I seat you at a stripy table and place a selection of food on a stripy plate for you?' James said.

'That would be wonderful. I shall of course view you as a failure if you do not manage to choose striped food for me. And I would expect you to match it to the plate.'

James laughed. 'Your word shall be my bidding.'

Once he'd seated her and was next to the buffet table, he realised that he had a dilemma: like the lovelorn juvenile he appeared to have become, he just wanted to rush straight back to Lady Maria, but he also wanted to impress her. Impress her with his food choices, though? Really? What was he becoming?

It was the first time in his life that he'd worked as fast as he could to match food to a plate but he did his best and soon he was back with Lady Maria. As he sat down, he was conscious of a lightening of his shoulders, a smile spreading across his face, really just a strong sense of *happiness*. Utterly ridiculous, really, because he didn't know her at all. By the end of this supper, he might have discovered that the two of them were extremely incompatible.

'I'm extremely impressed,' Lady Maria said. 'I had not thought you able to meet the challenge. I particularly like the way you have covered the food of the wrong colour with hams and asparagus to maintain the pink and green stripes without causing me to have too monotonous a meal.' The contrast between the seriousness of her tone and the laugh in her eyes was *adorable*.

As he grinned at her, and laughed, James was quite certain that he was not in fact going to find that they were incompatible.

As friends and companions, obviously. There would be no love involved.

Chapter Three

Anna

'I think you will find—' the duke leaned in as though he was about to impart extreme wisdom '—that the presentation of food in stripes to match a plate is one of the greatest challenges imaginable. Much greater, for example, than those undertaken by the dragon-slaying knights of yore.'

Anna laughed before inclining her head and saying with her best air of great seriousness, 'I think you're right. There is no ancient king who would not immediately reward such a knight with his daughter's hand.' She was enjoying herself immensely; she had never before in her life had this kind of conversation with an attractive man—other than the music master at her seminary in her last year of school, for which, when they were overheard by the Latin master, she had been roundly punished and the music master had not, which had not seemed very fair to her, but of course men and women were held to very different standards.

She was *very* glad that Maria and her godmother had persuaded her into attending this evening; she could be doing no harm to anyone and was having the most delightful time.

'If I were such a knight, I would be truly honoured to receive the hand of a maiden discerning enough to wish her food to be in stripes.' The duke looked directly into her eyes as he spoke, a half-smile playing about his lips. Anna felt her heart do a gigantic thump, and swallowed hard.

She and the duke were sitting close enough to each other that she could see the faint shadow where his beard growth was already restarting, the deep blue of his eyes, the thickness of his wavy dark hair. His shoulders were broad and she had the oddest feeling that if one allowed oneself to lay one's problems on those shoulders, one would be protected from the world. For a moment she felt a surge of real wistfulness when she thought of the fortunate young woman whom he would marry in due course.

Although, of course, he was probably just like all other men— kind and caring and dependable…until he wasn't.

At this moment, though, it was easy to imagine that he might be a rare, truly dependable man. She had had that impression of him from the very first moment she saw him; she'd been on the brink of laughter at the audacity of the deception she and her godmother were practising, and she'd felt so immediately comfortable with him that for one silly moment she'd almost confided in him.

They were still staring into each other's eyes, not speaking.

This would not do; she needed to look away, find some light words to cut across this…tension that she felt between them.

The duke was still gazing intently at her, and his smile was growing.

'I have so many questions for you,' he said.

'You do?' Anna's voice had emerged as a squeak.

'So many. I hope…' He paused for a moment, and his smile turned wry, almost as though he were laughing at himself. 'I hope that I may have the opportunity to get to know you well enough to ask them all.'

Anna swallowed again. She had no experience of meeting men in polite Society but she couldn't help feeling that—even though he knew nothing of her— the duke's flirting was in earnest. As though he was genuinely interested in getting to know her well.

Oh, of course: he was interested in getting to know *Lady Maria Swanley* well; as the daughter of an earl who was possessed of what Maria had confided was a truly enormous dowry, she would attract any number of suitors, including dukes, and that was exactly why Anna had not wished to attend this ball. She had *foreseen* this.

What Anna should probably do now was change the subject, converse on lighter matters, and certainly not flirt back. Except…

'*I* believe that I have a question for *you*,' she said, unable to resist the temptation. Although…what was her question? There were many things she would love to know about him, but all her questions would sound remarkably forward if she asked them now.

'I am all yours.' His smile was becoming ever more, well…intimate. As though it was just for her. 'Perhaps we could…*exchange*…questions.' The way he said it made Anna feel really quite warm, inside as well as out. It was almost as though he'd been about to say they could exchange…something else. 'A questions game, perhaps. She, or he, who can't think of another—sensible—question to ask on their turn, is the loser.'

'And what is the winner's reward?' she found herself asking.

'Perhaps that should be for the winner to decide?'

'I'm sure I will win.' Anna held his gaze and faux pursed her lips. She was quite sure that she shouldn't be conversing with the duke like this, but it was as though she was under some kind of compunction. Also, she never liked to turn down a challenge—which was, of course, partly why she was here in the first place; Maria had begun the whole charade by challenging Anna to take her place.

'I'm ready whenever you are. Ladies first.'

'Let me think.' Rational thought was quite difficult when she was sitting quite so close to the most intriguing and handsome man she'd ever met. 'If you were decorating a ballroom, how would you decorate it? Yourself. Not delegating to anyone else.'

Anna wasn't *very* pleased with her question, because it was a little dull, but it was better than nothing.

'Good question. In that it is one I have never before asked myself. I fear that my answer might disappoint you. I would aim for simplicity.'

Anna shook her head, mock sorrowfully. 'I am indeed disappointed. That is no answer.'

'You're right. I beg your pardon. I shall now apply myself to thinking of a better response. I do like the colour blue.'

'Better,' Anna approved. 'What kind of blue, though?'

'A mid blue. Similar to the sky on a summer's day, but a little darker.'

'That's a very nice colour. Stripes?'

'No stripes.' The duke looked into her eyes again and shook his own head. 'I must change my answer. I have just realised that my favourite colour is green. The green of your eyes.'

Anna chose to laugh. 'Now you are becoming ridiculous, Your Grace.'

'My name is James, and yes, I do fear that I am ridiculous. But at the same time...not.' His face was suddenly completely serious, and Anna was suddenly extremely breathless. 'Another colour that I now very much like,' he continued, 'is silver. The silver of your dress.' His gaze flickered lower, for the merest of seconds, to her chest, before returning to her face.

Anna came very close to repeating a very overcome *Oh!* before pulling herself together and saying, 'Would you have green and silver stripes?'

'I confess that I would not have stripes. I would instead decorate the entire ballroom in the green of your eyes and the entire supper room in silver spangles.'

'Would the green not feel a little monotonous?' Anna was *not* going to give in to the flutter in her stomach.

'Never. I feel it would be easy to look at the colour of your eyes every day for the rest of one's life.'

'If I had a fan, I would now rap you over the knuckles,' Anna told him, mock sternly. 'As you know, I was referring to the ballroom decorations. I feel, however, that we have exhausted this topic, and should move on.'

'Before I make further outrageous references to your beautiful eyes?'

'Exactly.'

'In that case, I believe that it's my turn for a question,' he said.

'I'm really not sure that I should grant it, considering how poor your response to my question was. I am, however, feeling generous.'

The duke's grin transformed his face from somewhat austere handsomeness into boyish cheekiness, and Anna was suddenly certain that she would remember this evening, this supper—and his grin—for the rest of her life.

'Thank you,' he said. 'So kind.'

She laughed.

'I have many, many questions,' he continued. 'It's difficult to choose. I will start with a small one. Of a different nature. What is your favourite food? Did I select well for you?'

'You did select well.' Anna had barely eaten a mouthful, she realised; she'd been too busy with their conversation. 'I like a lot of food; it's hard to choose a favourite.'

'No, no.' The duke shook his head. 'You are in danger of answering this question as badly as I answered yours.'

'Please accept my deepest apologies.'

'I will accept them *if* you answer the question properly.'

'That's very gracious of you, Your Grace.'

'James.'

Anna applied herself to deciding on her favourite food—asparagus and chicken—and then the duke (she really couldn't call him James) told her what his was—a most unimaginative steak, but he allowed that asparagus was delicious.

Eventually they decided that their question game had been a draw, and then their conversation—punctuated by mouthfuls of the most delectable food—continued in the same silly but utterly delightful vein until supper was ended.

Anna couldn't remember a time when she'd been more disappointed for a meal to finish. There was still, however, their waltz to look forward to. Although... she was beginning to be worried that for some strange reason the duke might like her for herself, rather than for Lady Maria's birth and connections, in which case would she be doing him a disservice to waltz with him? Maybe... But on the other hand, if he did enjoy her company, he would—perhaps she was flattering herself but he *might*—be sad not to see her again, and it probably wouldn't make much difference whether or not they shared another dance. Conversation, and getting to know each other a little, drew people together more than dancing, surely.

As he bowed deep over her hand when he released her to her partner for the next dance, a Mr Marsh, the duke said, 'I look forward to our waltz,' before raising his head and giving her that same intimate smile.

Anna was going to look forward with great anticipation to their dance.

As she walked towards the dance floor with Mr Marsh, she caught her godmother's eye. Lady Derwent was swivelling her eyes and jiggling her eyebrows in the most dramatic way.

'Would you mind if I spoke to my godmother for one moment before the dance?' she asked Mr Marsh.

'Certainly.'

'The duke is being most marked in his attentions,' Lady Derwent whispered as soon as Anna reached her side. 'There is every indication that he might wish to marry you.'

'Surely not.'

'Oh, I think so.'

'Well, I clearly can't marry him. I am about to become a governess.'

'Piffle. Your grandfather was the Earl of Broome, and Lady Puntney would certainly understand.'

'But I've lied to the duke. And I *am* ineligible. I mean, I'm sure it's moonshine anyway. But if it weren't, I wouldn't be able to.' And Anna had no interest in the institution of marriage; since men were not to be trusted to treat women well, she would probably be better off as a governess. At least she would have some independence and would not be relying on anyone other than her employer.

Lady Derwent wrinkled her brow and stared into the distance for a moment, and then said, 'I think on reflection that for the time being you are right. Now go and dance with Mr Marsh. He's delightful.'

'Thank you. Remember that we need to leave at midnight.' Anna could *not* be late tomorrow.

'Certainly. In the meantime, enjoy the rest of the evening.'

* * *

Mr Marsh was a very nice man, and Anna was determined to make the most of *every* dance this evening, not just the ones with the duke, because it was entirely possible that this was the only ball she would have the good fortune to attend in her entire life. But if she was honest, it was difficult not to be very aware of where the duke was at every moment—it was easy to see him because of his height—and also difficult not to fizz with anticipation ahead of her waltz with him.

She did enjoy dancing and some very nice conversation with Mr Marsh, and she was almost sorry to leave him at the end of the dance.

Except she wasn't really, because it was time for her second dance with the duke.

She had learnt the waltz during her seminary days, and earlier that day Lady Derwent had mangled one on the pianoforte while Lady Maria took the role of gentleman and led Anna round Lady Derwent's drawing room in a practice waltz. The practice had not gone well, due to Lady Maria's constantly forgetting that she was supposed to lead, but Anna was confident that she could remember the rudiments of the dance sufficiently accurately to acquit herself adequately this evening. Earlier, she and Lady Derwent had agreed out loud, so that others might hear, that she might waltz. She was quite sure that she was ready for the dance.

She had not, though, taken into account the way her heart would thud so very hard in her chest and that her anticipation of the duke's touch would cause her mind to falter.

'I've been looking forward to this dance,' the duke murmured as he took her in his arms.

Anna didn't trust her voice to come out sounding normal or indeed her mind to produce any sensible-sounding words, so she smiled and said nothing. How had she been naïve enough to think that a waltz would draw two people together less than conversation might?

Her senses were quite flooded by the duke, and in every way; he even *smelled* good. The only way she could describe his scent was just, well, *masculine*. A delightful kind of masculine. He *felt* good; his height and the width of his shoulders and the latent strength evident in his arms as he held her gave the impression of security and, again, extreme masculinity. Just *hardness*. And, of course, when she turned her face up to his, he *looked* good. His strong features and jawline, the way he looked harshly handsome in repose but delightfully cheekily handsome when he smiled... And the way his body looked in his perfectly fitting evening clothes.

The whole was just...magnificent. And, in this moment, she felt like the luckiest woman in the world. And, also, one of the least lucky, because nothing could ever come of her meeting the duke; this was for one evening only. She would remember it, however—perhaps be almost spoilt by it—for evermore.

Since it *was* for only one evening, she should *not* allow herself to feel maudlin; she should instead enjoy every last minute of this dance, and indeed the rest of the evening.

So she directed a huge smile in the duke's direction and sank into his hold. Her hand fitted perfectly inside his much larger one, and the way he was holding it made her almost shudder with delight. Although not as much as did the way his other hand rested lightly on her waist, and the way when they turned she sensed the hardness in his thighs and his chest. The way their bodies touched and moved together through the dance felt almost scandalous in its intimacy.

And then, as the duke led her through a turn, she looked up at his face, and if she'd already thought that this experience was intoxicating, well, she'd been wrong. What was truly intoxicating was the way he was looking at her now, as though they were the only two people in the world, as though with the half-smile on his lips he was making her some kind of promise, as though he saw deep inside her and very much admired what he saw.

Anna knew that she was being fanciful; from one smile one could hardly tell what a man was thinking. Perhaps he was just thinking that he liked the—really quite lovely—flowers that Lady Derwent had procured for her to wear in her hair, or perhaps he adored the waltz and smiled like that at everyone with whom he danced.

And then she stopped bothering to think, because it was far too much effort and definitely served no good purpose, and just gave herself up to enjoying the dance.

Some time later—she had no idea how long—she, or the duke, it was hard to tell, became aware of being jostled by others. She looked round and saw that the dance had come to an end. She was still held in the duke's strong arms, and he showed no sign of letting go of her yet, for which she could only be deeply grateful.

It defied belief, but somehow, over the course of this

short evening, it felt almost as though he had become very important to her, even though she barely knew him.

'That was…wonderful,' he said, still not releasing her.

'It was. I must thank you, very much.' She had a sudden mad wish to tell him the truth about herself, but, no, she couldn't; the secret was only half hers to impart, and, in addition, if he did choose to tell anyone else, or anyone overheard them, it could give rise to the most dreadful consequences.

'Would you like to take a turn outside on the balcony?' he asked, *still* not relaxing his hold on her. She in her turn, she realised, was still clinging onto him.

'I believe that I am taken for the next dance.'

'It is not for a few moments and, if you were to feel faint, I am sure the gentleman in question would release you from your commitment?'

'I *do* feel somewhat faint,' Anna agreed. It wasn't even entirely a lie; surely any lady would be feeling somewhat wobbly after being held quite so intimately for quite so long by a man like the duke.

'Then you must immediately get some fresh air.'

They were interrupted by an elderly man, who was powdered and painted in the way of the previous century. 'I believe that the next dance with Lady Maria is mine.'

The duke and Anna both moved a little way away from each other and dropped their arms. It was as though they had been in their own little universe and someone else had entered.

'Sir Richard. I'm afraid that you will have to excuse Lady Maria,' the duke told him, his demeanour suddenly quite haughty and even a little intimidating. 'She feels ill and is in need of fresh air.'

'I would be very happy to escort the lady myself to seek fresher air.'

'That is very kind, but I will perhaps return myself to my godmother,' Anna said. However much her mother had come from this world and however much at all levels of society men had rights that women did not, she still could not stand and listen to two men discussing what she was going to do next without attempting to interject.

'Certainly,' the duke said very promptly. 'I will escort you over to her.' He nodded to Sir Richard, whose face appeared to be purpling beneath his paint, and then somehow manoeuvred himself and Anna so that they were walking away from him.

'Would you like to return to Lady Derwent now or do you perhaps feel that you might be better served by breathing some fresher air first?'

Anna was quite sure that she ought just to return to her godmother, because would it not be quite scandalous for her to walk outside with the duke? But no one knew who she was, and she wouldn't see any of these people again at an occasion like this. No one would connect her with Lady Maria after this because they looked so different, and, anyway, Lady Maria would be getting married. And Anna's future employer—should they see her—which she did not think likely—would never recognise her in governess garb after seeing her dressed like this. And she so *very* much wanted to steal just a few more moments with the duke.

'Upon reflection,' she told him, 'I do believe that fresh air would serve me very well at this moment.'

As the duke made a way for them through the crowd, Anna allowed herself for this one moment to feel special, to relish these few minutes where he was effectively hers. The lady for whose hand he offered would be very lucky.

She thought for a moment of Maria. How could she possibly wish to marry Clarence, her curate, when she could presumably have had the duke at her feet? It would be remarkably easy to fall in love with the duke.

But of course Maria had already fallen in love, and Anna had to admire her bravery; very few young ladies would have the courage to choose to marry someone in Clarence's straitened circumstances. Although Anna's own mother had of course been much braver than that: she had married her father's second groom. Anna hoped Maria was making the right decision; in the case of her parents, their difference in stations and the change in her mother's circumstances upon her elopement had put a strain upon her parents' relationship until eventually her father had left.

'You look as though you're thinking about something very serious,' the duke said as they stepped out of the long glass doors leading to a terrace along the back of the house. 'Please don't feel that you have to walk out here with me if you do not wish to; I would be more than happy to return you immediately to Lady Derwent.'

'Oh, no, I am very happy. That is…if you would still like to walk?'

'Very happy indeed,' he murmured, which made Anna smile.

As they moved along the terrace, he said, 'We are fortunate in having a particularly nice rose garden. Down those steps.' He pointed ahead. 'Would you like to take a walk around it? The moonlight and clear skies allow us to see quite well tonight.'

'I should very much like to, thank you.'

They continued towards the steps, Anna holding the duke's arm, and he said, 'I realise now that I was dreadfully short-sighted in not asking you what your favourite flowers were when we were asking questions of each other.'

'Fortunately, roses are some of my favourites.'

'Mine too,' he said. 'What a happy coincidence.'

Anna laughed; it was as though her senses were so heightened at this moment that the tiniest joke must seem hilarious.

'Take care on the steps,' the duke instructed. 'They are quite uneven and guests have been known to fall on them even in broad daylight. Allow me to hold your arm a little more tightly.'

Anna was more than happy to have her arm held more tightly. In fact, she couldn't think of anything she'd like more right now than to be held tightly by the duke.

'Thank you,' she said, a little breathlessly.

It was most enjoyable descending the steps clamped hard against his side. Anna couldn't believe that it was necessary for him to hold her steady with quite so much determination, but she certainly wasn't going to quibble. She had determined to enjoy this evening, and proximity to him could only enhance her enjoyment.

The steps safely negotiated, the duke drew her left. In the hazy light, Anna made out an archway into a walled garden, and then a profusion of rose bushes, laid out in a very regular fashion.

'These are indeed beautiful,' she said. 'I very much

like seeing a gardener's work: the love and care put into the planting and nurturing of the plants.'

'I agree, although in truth our head gardener, Alliss, whilst very talented, is a very grumpy individual who would be most put out if anyone suspected him of putting love into his work.'

Anna laughed. 'I refuse to believe that no love has gone into this planting. Look at them. They're wonderful. Quite beautiful.'

'Mmm.' The duke was not looking at the roses; he was looking at her. 'You are also very beautiful,' he told her, his voice completely serious. 'Your smile is… perfection.'

Anna felt his words to the very core of her body, and swallowed, suddenly suffused with emotion. While she had been educated as though she would one day take her place in Society and she was now two-and-twenty years old, quite old enough to know the ways of the world, she had no idea to what extent men spoke to women like this just for fun. Lady Maria was a young lady of quality, though, and chaperoned by Lady Derwent, and the duke was under his own roof. It seemed quite unlikely that he would attempt to take advantage of her; it seemed possible therefore that he really might mean his words. For the moment, at least.

Perhaps she should tell him now who she really was; being here under false pretences was beginning to feel terrible. But no, she'd already been over this in her mind, and she couldn't. It was not Anna's secret to share; she would be betraying Maria.

'Would you care to sit down?' the duke asked.

'There's a bench over there in the corner, with a lovely view of some of the better rose bushes.'

'That sounds delightful,' Anna said primly. She would tell him *something* to ensure that he was not led into believing she could be courted. And she would enjoy his conversation. And then she would leave.

She gasped as she sat down; the stone was very cold against her skin through her thin dress.

'I'm so sorry,' the duke said immediately. 'I should have been more considerate. Allow me to warm you with my jacket.'

'Oh, no, I... *Oh*!'

The duke had immediately divested himself of his jacket and placed it around her shoulders, and it was the most wonderful sensation being enveloped in his clothing, his scent again and the warmth from where his body had just been touching it.

'May I...?' He lifted his arm as though to place it around Anna's shoulders. She was fairly sure that she should say no, but she couldn't quite remember why. It wasn't as though a gentleman placing his arm around one's shoulders was *kissing*, after all.

So she smiled at him, and he smiled back at her, and hugged her into him.

And this felt even more intimate than their waltz had, because now they really *were* alone, rather than just feeling as though they were.

She had no idea what might happen next, but she was aware that, even though she barely knew him, she did trust the duke. Which was ridiculous, of course, because all she really knew of men from first-hand experience was that they were not to be trusted.

'Where is your childhood home?' he asked. 'Is it similar to London or very different?'

'It is in Somerset, and very different from London.' Anna had grown up in Gloucestershire, but Lady Maria's family home was quite close to Bath. Anna knew it reasonably well, having been invited to stay with her best friend on three occasions.

'Oh, yes, you mentioned that you had been enjoying visiting the sights of London. What do you have planned for tomorrow?'

'Tomorrow, I… I think…' Anna suddenly had a large lump in her throat at the mention of the next day. Tomorrow she would be leaving behind any pretence that this life could possibly be for her, and moving into the Puntneys' home before beginning her employment in earnest the following day.

'I ask…' The duke shifted a little on the bench so that, while still keeping his arm around Anna's shoulders, he was now also facing her. 'I ask because I should very much like to call on you tomorrow.'

'Oh!' *Oh.* Oh, no. This wasn't the way Anna had foreseen the deception going wrong, but it definitely *was* wrong.

The duke was looking—gazing—at her in the most *exciting* way and all she could do was swallow.

'I would like to take you for a drive in Hyde Park.' He lifted the hand that was not around Anna's shoulders, and very gently traced the curve of her cheek with one finger, which caused Anna's breath to hitch. 'I would also like to take you for a drive in Richmond Park.' He moved a little closer. Anna could hardly remember how to breathe. 'And I would like to show you around my estates.' He moved even closer. 'Further, I would like to assist your godmother in showing you as many of the sights of London that you would like to see.'

He drew her a little closer to him with his arm, and moved his free hand so that it was in Anna's curls, cupping the back of her neck.

'I would like—' the duke's voice was low and husky now, and every word he spoke sent a shiver through Anna '—to do so many things with you. I know that we've only just met but I feel...' He paused and then continued, 'I'm sorry. That's far too much. To begin with.' He tugged her hair very slightly, very gently, so that her head was angled exactly beneath his. And then, very, very slowly, he leaned towards her and brushed her lips with his. 'I would very much like to call on you tomorrow.'

'I would like that too, but...' Anna barely knew what she was saying. She was very aware that she had to tell him something *now* so that he wouldn't be holding any misconceptions, but she was even more aware of how he was holding her and where his lips had just touched hers.

'That.' The duke brushed her lips again with his, for a little longer this time. Anna's heart was beating *so* hard. 'Is.' He dropped another kiss on her lips and Anna wondered through the mists of feeling whether she might explode with...something. 'Wonderful.'

And then he kissed her for longer. And then he parted her lips with his tongue, and Anna felt it throughout her entire body. And then she found herself kissing him back, and it was truly, truly the most delicious thing she'd ever done in her entire life.

Anna had no idea how long they kissed for. She was

dimly aware of being held tightly by the duke, one of his arms now sliding around her waist, of winding her own arms around his neck and then plunging her hands into his hair.

When they eventually stopped the kiss, the duke took a deep breath and then just held her very tightly, his cheek against her hair. Being in his arms felt like the most natural place in the world to be, as though she *should* be there. Which was odd, because in reality she hardly knew him, and she was here with him under extreme false pretences.

As she thought that, she snuggled even more closely against him, wanting this moment to go on for ever.

And then, to her great disappointment, the duke planted a kiss on her forehead and drew back, easing his hold on her.

'We should be careful,' he said, his voice ragged. 'I could… I could… We could… We must not do things that a young lady should not do outside marriage. And to that end…' He moved a little further away and took his arm away from her.

'I would like to call on you tomorrow,' he said firmly. 'Much as I would like to stay out here, I think we should go back inside now. I do not trust myself to avoid temptation.'

Anna was going to have to tell him. As soon as possible.

She needed to find the words.

'I should give your jacket back to you,' she said first.

'When we are closer to the house. Otherwise, you will catch cold.'

'Thank you.'

They stood up and began to retrace their steps towards the building.

'I have enjoyed this evening very greatly,' the duke said as they walked.

'So have I. Thank you. It has been one of the most enjoyable of my life.' Anna knew that she would treasure the memory; she also knew that she would find it hard not to wish that he really could have called on her tomorrow.

When he pressed her hand on his arm and she smiled up at him in the moonlight, she suddenly felt quite tearful at the tender look on his face.

They were nearly at the terrace now.

'I must return your jacket to you,' she told him.

As he helped her out of it, his hands lingered for just a little longer than necessary on her bare arms, and she shivered through the entire length of her body in response.

'Thank you.' Honestly, her voice sounded quite tremulous.

She now felt very cold. Not just physically, but emotionally. As though the most wonderful interlude in her life had finished and it would take her a long time to feel warm again.

They trod up the steps and along the path together, Anna keeping her eyes fixed straight ahead because she couldn't bear to look at the duke.

And then, just before they stepped back inside the ballroom, she moved away from him and said, 'I'm so sorry, but I think I return to the country soon and will not be able to see you again.'

She looked up at him for a second and saw him just staring, and slightly frowning.

He reached a hand out to her and, ridiculously, because in reality she'd only known him for a few short hours, she felt as though her heart might break.

'Goodbye,' she said. 'Thank you so very much for a truly wonderful evening. Quite the best evening of my life. I have enjoyed it so very much.'

And then she walked away as fast as she could.

Chapter Four

James

James awoke slowly the next morning, from a dream where he'd been chasing something—maybe a butterfly—that he couldn't quite catch. He lay blinking for a few moments, conscious of a strong sense of dissatisfaction, waiting for clarity of thought to return, and then suddenly he remembered. Last night. Lady Maria. The strong sense of connection they'd shared, or he'd thought they'd shared. And then…her disappearance.

He pushed back his covers and swung his legs out of bed; he felt as though he had a lot to do.

Although, he realised, as he shook his head to clear it fully, it was far too early to pay a call on anyone. And he wasn't entirely sure that Lady Maria would *like* him to call on her. He couldn't decide which was the greater indicator: her sudden flight or the fact that she'd told him that yesterday evening had been wonderful, the best of her life.

He called for water and soap, still shaking his head

a little, wondering what exactly had happened to him yesterday evening.

Before the ball, if he'd been asked, he'd have said that he expected that at some point he would come to a sensible, measured decision regarding the choice of young lady to whom he would offer his hand in marriage. He had not had any real idea about how he might make that decision but he did know that he hadn't expected to know for certain after one evening—perhaps one minute—which lady he would choose.

He had also not expected that if he *did* meet someone with whom he could imagine spending his life, someone with whom he could enjoy companionship and friendship, he would be unlucky enough for the young lady to tell him that she would be leaving for the country and unable to see him again.

Had she meant it? He just didn't know.

He washed and dressed hurriedly—although he did take the time to ensure that his cravat fell well, in the hope that he would be able to speak to Lady Maria later—still with the strong sense that he was in a rush to take some kind of action, and then descended to the breakfast parlour.

As he sat to eat steak—which reminded him of eating supper with Lady Maria—he tried to marshal his thoughts.

The contrast between her telling him she was leaving for the country and that she wouldn't be able to see him again and the way she'd melted into the crowd of guests so quickly that he hadn't been able to follow her, and the fact that she'd told him with seeming great sincerity how very much she'd enjoyed the evening, was very confusing.

Perhaps she hadn't really meant that she wouldn't be able to see him again; perhaps she had just meant that when she left for the country she would be residing far from London and didn't expect to see him again *easily*. Or soon.

Perhaps she'd been as overwhelmed as he by the connection and tension there had been between them and had panicked a little. Perhaps she had thought he was merely trifling with her. She was certainly not experienced with men; he had had the strongest sense when he kissed her that it was the first time she had kissed anyone or been kissed like that.

He took a large swig of ale and frowned a little as he considered how he would plan his day.

It wasn't difficult, actually.

He *knew* that he wanted to marry Lady Maria. He needed to get married. He hadn't wanted to get married. He didn't wish to fall in love and he didn't wish anyone to fall in love with him. But they weren't in love. How could they be when they barely knew each other? They had merely experienced an intense connection of the sort that he could easily imagine would lead to an excellent understanding and partnership between them. And the intimate side of marriage would certainly be no hardship with Lady Maria. She would make the ideal bride for him.

And therefore he would like to propose to her today.

She would surely not be leaving for the country as soon as this morning, unless she had had word that her grandmother had taken a turn for the worse.

So he would pay a call on her as early as he reasonably could and hope very much that the reason that she had effectively run away from him last night was merely that she had felt overwhelmed by what had happened and had not understood that his intentions were serious and entirely honourable, and that she would accept his proposal.

And between now and then he should really do his best to do something better with his day than just kick his heels in impatience.

He achieved very little other than a ludicrous amount of pacing before the hour at which he might call on Lady Maria finally arrived.

He had sent a footman to enquire about where she was residing, given that her mother had left town, and had been told that she was staying in her own home, accompanied by two very elderly great-aunts. Their age would presumably explain why she had been accompanied last night by Lady Derwent.

Standing on the doorstep of the Grosvenor Square house, he found his hands going to his cravat to check it more than once, and realised that he was squaring his shoulders and taking deeper breaths than he might usually do.

The door was opened by a particularly stately butler, who showed him into a conservatively decorated parlour to the left of the hall.

James sat and then stood and then sat and then stood again as he waited.

And then, finally, the door opened and the butler announced Lady Maria and her aunt, Lady Sephranella.

The first lady to enter the room was aged and walked slowly with a stick. James greeted her politely, looking eagerly beyond her to where Lady Maria would appear.

The young lady who followed her into the room was not, however, Lady Maria.

He turned to Lady Sephranella, not wishing to be rude to whomever this young lady might be. Perhaps a cousin of Lady Maria's.

'I wondered whether I might be able to see Lady Maria,' he said.

'I am Lady Maria,' the younger lady said.

James frowned. 'I'm afraid I don't understand,' he said. This young lady was tall and blond-haired and blue-eyed, whereas the Lady Maria that he had met was smaller, brown-haired and green-eyed. This lady was beautiful, but his Lady Maria was *really* beautiful. Especially when she smiled. 'I wondered whether I might be able to see Lady Maria Swanley.'

'I am Lady Maria Swanley.' She spoke very slowly, as if to someone who did not have strong comprehension.

James shook his head.

'I met Lady Maria last night,' he said. 'Lady Maria Swanley.'

'Really?' The lady in front of him shook her own head. 'I'm so sorry but I don't entirely remember. It was of course a great crush—so wonderful that the whole world wished to attend your mama's ball—so one met a great many people. It is difficult to remember to whom one spoke.'

James frowned at her. She looked absolutely nothing like the actual Lady Maria. The only thing this lady and *his* Lady Maria had in common, he realised, was that this one's eyes seemed to be dancing with merriment, as his Lady Maria's had last night when he met her.

He… What? Could they… What?

Could they have played some kind of trick on him, on the *ton*? Surely not? *Why*? There had to be some other explanation. This Lady Maria really did look, however, as though she was on the brink of laughter.

'I am the Duke of Amscott,' he said.

'Yes,' agreed the lady.

'Last night, my mother held a ball.'

'Yes.'

'At the ball, I met and danced twice with Lady Maria Swanley.'

'I am Lady Maria Swanley.'

'I do not, however—' James was starting to find it difficult to get his words out without shouting '—recall having met you before.'

The lady cast her eyes down. 'I must confess that I would be a little hurt by your words, Your Grace, were it not for the fact that I do not easily recall you either.'

'Are you indeed Lady Maria Swanley?' James asked baldly, ignoring her last sentence.

'Yes, of course I am.' The lady's smile was so bland as to be suspicious.

'Are you confused, Your Grace?' Lady Sephranella quavered from the corner of the room. 'This is my great-niece, the granddaughter of my sister. This is Lady Maria Swanley. Have you come to the wrong house, sir?'

Could it be possible that the elderly lady and the butler were both colluding in a plot to pretend that this lady was Lady Maria? Why on earth would they do that? They *couldn't* be.

He took another long look at the lady who called herself Lady Maria. She was still smiling blandly at him and her eyes were still dancing. She looked ridiculously mischievous.

'I have not come to the wrong house but I will bid you good afternoon.' Clearly, he needed to go and see Lady Derwent.

Twenty minutes later, he was waiting in a grand drawing room in Lady Derwent's Berkeley Square mansion, which, coincidentally, was directly opposite his own, on the other side of the gardens in the middle of the square.

'Your Grace.' Lady Derwent swept into the room in a rustle of stiff silk.

'My Lady.'

Greetings dispensed with, James came straight to the point. 'I would very much like to pay a call on Lady Maria Swanley today.'

'I believe that Lady Maria resides in Grosvenor Square.'

'She is not here?'

Lady Derwent raised her eyebrows. 'No?'

James had rarely in his life spent so much time in one afternoon wishing to grind his teeth. 'Yesterday evening, at my mother's ball, you introduced your goddaughter, Lady Maria Swanley, to me.'

'That is correct.' Lady Derwent moved to a chair near the fireplace and said, 'Please sit down.'

'Thank you. I enjoyed meeting Lady Maria.'

'We enjoyed attending the ball; thank you so much. I particularly liked the decorations. I believe that your mama will have created a fashion.'

'Thank you. Indeed.' James did not wish to discuss ballroom furnishings. 'I am a little confused. I have just been to call on Lady Maria at her house.'

'How very pleasant.'

'The Lady Maria that I met at her house was not the Lady Maria that I met last night.'

'Did you visit the correct Lady Maria? Maria is quite a common name.'

James had to work hard not to grind his teeth. 'Yes. I understand from you that the lady I met last night was Lady Maria Swanley. And the lady I visited today was Lady Maria Swanley. They were not, however, the same person.'

Lady Derwent inclined her head to one side and frowned slightly. 'I myself am also now confused. How could that be? I was not aware that there were two Lady Maria Swanleys.'

'I am sure there are not.'

'Then I do not understand what you mean.'

'Last night—' James was surprised that he was not now yelling '—I met a Lady Maria Swanley, whom you introduced as your goddaughter. I danced twice with her, I ate supper with her, I conversed with her.' He had *kissed* her.

Lady Derwent nodded. 'Yes.'

'And this afternoon I went to call on Lady Maria Swanley, at her house. A young lady came into the room where I was waiting. The butler and a Lady Sephranella, described to me as Lady Maria's great-aunt, referred to the young lady as Lady Maria Swanley. She referred to herself as Lady Maria Swanley. She said that she had been at the ball and thought that she had probably met me but did not remember me. I did not remember her at all because I have never met her before because she was not *my* Lady Maria Swanley.'

'*Your* Lady Maria Swanley?'

'I had—' James was aware that he had lost all dignity and he did not care '—that is to say, I formed quite an attachment to Lady Maria over the course of yesterday evening. I wished to call on her today to further our acquaintance.'

'I see.' Lady Derwent looked thoughtful.

'Forgive me if I appear rude.' James did not care at all if he appeared rude right now. 'I wonder if you could explain what has happened. Where is the Lady Maria I met last night and what relation does she have to the Lady Maria I met this afternoon?'

Lady Derwent placed her hands together, palm to palm, and touched them to her chin for a moment, before relaxing her fingers so that they clasped each other and laying her hands in her lap.

Speaking slowly, as though choosing her words carefully, she said, 'I believe that you met Lady Maria Swanley this afternoon.'

'Who was the lady I met yesterday evening then?'

Lady Derwent paused for a moment and then said, 'Lady Maria Swanley.' She turned and rang the bell next to her. 'Would you like to take tea?'

James looked at her for a long moment and then said, 'Thank you; I am afraid that I have urgent business to attend to and must leave.'

Lady Derwent nodded. 'Do visit again.'

'I should be delighted.' James just wanted to swear.

* * *

Marching away from Lady Derwent's house, James had the strangest sensation that his head was going to explode. Someone—everyone—had to be lying to him, because clearly at least one of the two purported Lady Marias was not the real one. But *why* were they lying?

Something was nagging at the edge of his mind. As his thoughts began to crystallise, he stopped dead in the middle of the pavement, and a little boy out with his nurse for a walk ran right into him.

'I do apologise,' James said, his mind working hard.

Both so-called Lady Marias had seemed mirthful on his first meeting with them. It was easy to imagine that the mirth might have related to a secret. And that that secret might be the impersonation by one of the ladies of the other.

The first Lady Maria had *known* that she was going to be meeting people that evening, in the guise of Lady Maria. The second Lady Maria had not known until he arrived that James would call on her today. Had the first Lady Maria been the real one, she would not have been mirthful about the masquerade that neither she nor the second Lady Maria could know might arise, as neither would have known at that point that he would make to-day's call.

Of course, the mirth might have been for a different reason.

But logic suggested that if one of the two ladies was impersonating Lady Maria, and they both knew about it, which they must do, and that was what had caused both ladies' mirth, it was the second lady who was the real one, and last night's Lady Maria who was the fake.

He turned round. He was going back to see Lady Derwent again.

'What a delightful surprise,' said Lady Derwent five minutes later, indicating that James should take a chair near to hers. 'I had not thought to see you again so soon, Your Grace.'

'No, indeed; this is very soon,' agreed James, sitting as directed. 'I will not take up too much of your time. I have merely come to say that I believe that the lady I met yesterday evening under the guise of Lady Maria Swanley was not in fact Lady Maria. I must apologise for any implied rudeness—' he bowed '—but it seems to me that you were aware of the deception.'

Lady Derwent studied him for a long moment, and then said, in much milder tones than she usually used, 'That would of course be an astonishing deception. Quite unbelievable, in fact; ladies such as I do not practise such deceptions.'

She was clearly lying.

James leaned forward. 'Who was the lady I met last night?'

Lady Derwent shook her head, a little sorrowfully, and said, 'Lady Maria Swanley.'

James tried not to roll his eyes and failed. 'I should be very grateful if you would pass on a message to the lady I met last night.'

'What kind of message would you like to pass on to... Lady Maria?'

'I...' James could not just blurt out a marriage proposal by proxy. 'I… I would very much like the opportunity to see again the lady that I met last night.'

'That is not a particularly interesting sentiment.' Lady Derwent sounded a little disappointed. 'Perhaps a stronger message would have a greater effect.'

James narrowed his eyes. Was she *encouraging* him to make serious advances? How very peculiar. Had she somehow orchestrated his meeting with last night's Lady Maria so that he would propose to her? No. That was preposterous. She could not possibly have known that he would be captivated by one smile, and she was hardly making it easy for him to see her now.

'If I am able to see her again, I am sure that I will have a stronger message for her,' he said.

Lady Derwent inclined her head graciously. 'I will bear that in mind.'

Three days later, James was taking tea with his mother and sisters, his mood still fairly bleak.

He realised now that it was a good thing that the young lady he had met had disappeared; he had to admit that some would describe the level of infatuation he had experienced as close to having fallen head over heels in love on first sight, and he did not wish to fall in love. He was beginning to come to terms with the loss of his father and brothers, and he did not wish to experience further loss. Women died in childbirth all the time, for example. And if the lady reciprocated his feelings and he did die young like his brothers, that would be terrible for her.

So, yes, with hindsight, he was inclined—when reflecting rationally—to think he'd had a lucky escape.

He could have been in danger of falling in love, and love was a dangerous emotion. Really, it was a good thing that he was unable to get to know the lady any better or propose marriage to her. He was quite convinced of it.

It was more difficult, however, to convince himself that he was feeling particularly happy or that life was particularly enjoyable. Stupidly, given that he did not know the lady at all—hell, he didn't even know her real *name*—he felt that he missed her. In addition, there was clearly an unsolved mystery surrounding her identity that he would have liked to have solved. And he didn't *think* she could be in any kind of trouble, given that she had been under Lady Derwent's protection, but he wasn't *certain* that all was well with her.

He had considered paying a detective to look for her, but rationally felt that he should not. He could not *force* her to tell him who she was.

'Ouch.'

His mother had just rapped him across the knuckles.

'James,' she tutted. 'You have been paying very little heed to us this afternoon. You appear to be wrapped up in thoughts of your own.'

'My apologies, Mama. I am a little tired.'

'You should get more sleep. We were discussing which young ladies you are considering getting to know better with marriage in mind.'

James suddenly felt very tired. 'I am not sure that I wish to marry soon.'

His mother frowned. 'I thought we had already discussed this.'

James sighed. In truth, they *had* discussed it, and he did have to produce an heir while he was still in good health. He'd been over this in his mind countless times now. He absolutely did not wish to marry someone with whom he was in love or who loved him. It was for the best that Lady Maria—or whoever she had been—had disappeared. As long as she was in good health, happy and safe. *No.* He was not going to start worrying about this again.

He took a deep breath and turned to his mother. 'Whom do you suggest I meet?'

Two days later, James and his mother called on a very pleasant young lady, a Lady Catherine Rainsford, a mar-chioness's daughter with a large dowry, a pretty face and easy but not overwhelming conversation.

On their return home, his mother pulled her gloves off and handed them to their butler.

'Lady Catherine is a delightful young lady.' She walked into the smaller of the two saloons leading right off the hall, her demeanour very much indicating that she expected James to follow. 'Do you think that you might like to marry her?'

'I…' James really had no idea whom he might like to marry. Well, he had an idea whom he would *like* to marry, but not whom he *would* marry. 'She does seem very pleasant.' He could certainly imagine being friends with her. 'And quite attractive.' He *supposed* he could imagine making love to her.

It was probably *good* that he didn't feel terribly ex-cited by that. As he had told himself many times be-fore, he did not want to be in love with his wife, and he didn't think he would fall in love with Lady Catherine. And she really would be very suitable. She was well-formed. Not too tall, not too small. She had a nice face and nice hair. She seemed reasonably intelligent but not a bluestocking. He presumed that she would be a good mother for his children.

Really, he couldn't imagine a better wife.

Except, well, he *could*...

This was ridiculous.

What had his mother asked? Whether he might like to marry her.

'Perhaps I might,' he said.

'James.' His mother's hand went to her mouth, and then she reached up and hugged him before releasing him and patting her hair in the mirror. 'Darling, I'm quite excited.'

'So am I,' he told her untruthfully.

'When will you propose to her?'

'Soon. I think. Although, I am not certain.'

'Oh.' His mother plumped herself down on a chair as though all the stuffing had suddenly gone out of her. 'I do think you should marry soon, my dear.'

James nodded. 'I know. I will.' He looked at his mother. He loved her and his sisters very much. He did need to ensure that their future was secure, and for that he did need at least one son. 'Soon. I just need a little time to get used to the idea.'

'Darling, if you don't feel comfortable marrying, please don't let me push you into it.'

James raised his eyebrows wryly. 'Really?'

'Yes. I'm aware that I have indeed been trying to persuade you into it, but I believe that you would be happy, should you find a young woman with whom you were compatible. I would be delighted for you if you came

to love her as deeply as I loved your father.' She and
James's father had had an arranged marriage that had
turned out to be a very happy one. 'I thought... I wondered whether you were singling out Lady Maria Swanley at our ball, but you haven't mentioned her since then.'
She had mentioned Lady Maria obliquely once or twice
since the ball but this was the first time she had mentioned her explicitly.

'Yes. No. I haven't, no. She...left London.'

'Oh, I know why.' James's sister Charlotte had come
into the room and caught the latest part of their conversation. 'Have you not heard the latest *on-dit*? Lady Maria
has become engaged to a penniless curate, although he
is of very good birth, I believe. Her mama is very unhappy about it, but I have it from dearest Eliza Feath-
erley that because Lady Maria is now twenty-one she
is old enough to make her own decision and intends to
marry and retire to the country with him. He has a living in Hampshire.'

'Really!' their mother said.

Really, James thought. If this had been going on for
some time, perhaps that was why Lady Maria had practised her deception. Perhaps she had sent a friend to the
ball in her place because she did not wish to participate
in the Season's marriage mart when she was already
promised to her fiancé. But why would Lady Derwent
have colluded in that?

'What is it about Lady Derwent that you don't like?'
he asked his mother.

'We know each other well but we've never really been
good friends. We came out in the same year and she
nearly ran away with your dear father, before he saw

sense and married me. She's always been quite wild. Even now. She acts the grand Society matron on one hand but on the other does not have a great regard for convention.'

'Very interesting.' Very interesting indeed.

They attended a musical soirée together that evening, because James's mother had ascertained that Lady Catherine would be there.

Shortly after they arrived, James looked round to discover Lady Derwent at his elbow. It seemed very much as though she was there by design. Perhaps she had more to say about Lady Maria.

'I wondered if you might be able to procure some lemonade for me,' she said.

When he had the drink, he found her sitting in a corner, waiting for him.

'Thank you.' She took the glass from him and patted the empty chair next to her. 'Do sit and keep me company for a moment.'

'Of course.'

James was barely seated before she said, 'I believe that you would find it of interest to walk near the cows' pasture in the north-west part of Hyde Park in the morning. At perhaps eleven o'clock.'

James raised his eyebrows. Presumably this had something to do with the fake Lady Maria.

'Indeed?' he asked.

'I am thinking about our last conversation,' she pursued. 'I would recommend that you take a walk there before coming to any important decisions.'

'For a particular purpose?' he asked.

'Eleven o'clock,' she repeated, as though he had not spoken.

'I will bear that in mind,' he said, blinking.

'Are you a musical devotee?' she asked.

'Erm, no.'

'Never mind.' She smiled at him and then launched into a description of the renowned soprano who was going to be singing to them shortly.

James nodded and said very little—he had no opinions to offer on the soprano in question—until eventually Lady Derwent said, 'You must go and find your mother. Don't forget. Eleven o'clock. Tomorrow.'

As James bent his head over her hand, he had no idea whether he would take himself to Hyde Park on the morrow or not.

He still wasn't entirely sure whether he would go to Hyde Park the next day, he told himself, as he endured a lengthy monologue from Lady Catherine on the subject of music, wondering the whole time whether he really would like to be married to her, and unable to stop thinking about Lady Maria—*his* Lady Maria—and wondering whether her presence would have made this evening more enjoyable (he was quite sure that it would).

He would not yet propose marriage to Lady Catherine. He needed to think a little more about it.

He was always going to have come to Hyde Park, he reflected fourteen hours later, as he walked his horse, Star, down the path that led to the spot that Lady Derwent had described to him the previous evening. Of course he was. As he'd listened to a succession of warbling sopranos and growling tenors, he'd reflected on

the conversations that he'd had with her and had concluded that of course her suggestion—command—had
something to do with his Lady Maria.

And if Lady Derwent was trying to arrange a meeting between him and the fake Lady Maria he couldn't
resist attending.

When he came upon the clearing that Lady Derwent
had mentioned, he found that there was no one there.
His pocket watch told him that it was still five minutes
before eleven.

The next few minutes passed unutterably slowly as
he walked Star round, just waiting to see what would
happen.

When he did eventually hear people approaching, he
turned quickly, only to see that it was not Lady Maria.

Rather, the little group that was approaching com-
prised three children, a nursemaid and a grey-clad lady
who was presumably a governess.

James's gaze rested on the group very briefly, before
he resumed looking around to see if other people—in
particular a small lady with a beautiful smile—might
be approaching. And then, he could not say why, he
found his eyes being drawn back to the little group, and
in particular to the lady in grey. There was something
about her…

He looked hard at her and, as he stared, her head
turned in his direction, and she gave a noticeable start.

He hadn't been able to make out her features fully,
due to the bonnet she was wearing and the fact that on
glimpsing him she had then turned away, and yet he had
the strongest feeling…

Was she…?

He dismounted, looped Star's reins around a tree and strode over to the group.

'Good morning,' he said, directing his words at the grey-clad woman. His accosting the group was of course somewhat irregular, but he felt a strong compulsion to confirm his suspicions.

'Good morning.' She kept her head lowered so that it was difficult to see her face, but her voice was recognisable, and so was her posture. Good God.

'Lady Maria!' he exclaimed.

She froze and then, after a long moment, looked up at him.

If he wasn't mistaken, her eyes were filling. Surprisingly, given that surely *she* had wronged *him*, he found himself feeling guilty.

'I'm afraid that you are mistaken,' she told him, shaking her head. There was no trace of her smile. 'Good morning. We must be on our way.'

'No,' he blurted out. He felt as though he *needed* to find out more about her. And Lady Derwent had clearly meant him to find this lady, whoever she really was. As though in some way they were *intended* to meet again.

The lady tilted her head very slightly to one side and said, 'No?' Her tone was significantly frostier than he had assumed her capable of.

Which was arguably quite ridiculous given that *she* had lied to *him*.

'I should be very grateful if you would afford me a few moments of your time,' he said.

'I...' She took a deep breath and then glanced over her shoulder at the nurse and children behind her. 'I am unfortunately busy.'

'Please?' Apparently he was begging. Which, again, felt quite ridiculous. 'Just a minute or two?'

She looked into his face for quite a long time before pressing her lips together and saying, 'One moment.' She turned to the maid and said, 'Elsie, I should be grateful if you would take the children for a short walk along the path over there. Children, please could you look at the different leaves on the trees and try to ascertain what type of tree they are?'

James waited a few moments so that the remainder of her party would be out of earshot, and then said in a low voice, so that they would not hear, 'I would appreciate an explanation. I take it that you masqueraded as Lady Maria at the ball.'

'Yes, I did. I am sorry if I offended you in any way.' She gave a small nod, as though to end the conversation, and took a step or two away from him.

'I don't think this is the end of the conversation,' James stated. How could she possibly think that it was acceptable to practise such an outrageous deception—in his house—and admit to it but behave as though that would be the end of it? At the very least, surely, she should tell him why. And apologise. And…

Well, he didn't know what else. He couldn't really work out how he felt about her any more.

Good God, he'd been on the brink of *proposing* to her. And she was… Well, he had no idea who she was. She was a governess. Who'd been pretending to be Lady Maria Swanley. The whole thing was preposterous.

Perhaps the personality she had presented to him had also been fake. He wasn't sure whether that thought made him feel angry or sad or... Maybe confused. And, yes, definitely angry.

'I would suggest that you owe me an explanation,' he told her.

'I...' She stopped and turned back to face him fully, before saying, 'Yes. The explanation is not entirely mine to give, however. Lady Maria and I are very close friends. Lady Derwent is my godmother. Lady Maria did not wish to attend the ball for reasons of her own, which I cannot disclose, and she asked me to go in her place. Lady Derwent persuaded me that it would be a good idea to enjoy one ball before I began my employment here. I beg of you not to tell my employer that I undertook the masquerade.'

'Your employer?'

'I am a governess.'

Of course. That explained the grey dress. And the children. It did not explain how Lady Derwent was her godmother and Lady Maria her good friend.

'I will not tell your employer.' He was still very angry but he had no taste for vindictiveness. 'I would ask, however: did none of you think of the consequences of your action? I cannot understand how any of you would think that it was an acceptable thing to do. It was rude, it was ridiculous, it was preposterous, it was *stupid*.'

'I'm sorry, I...' she began. And then she stopped and pressed her lips together and tilted her head slightly. 'I do understand that Society might not look kindly on such a masquerade. However, I am sure that it is rare for two people to meet and make a strong connection on such an occasion. Had I just danced and talked to a succession of different people that evening, and then disappeared, no one would have been any the wiser. Whilst I would have had one very enjoyable evening. I believe that your disapprobation is perhaps due to the fact that you and I spent a long time talking and that you feel that I misled you.'

James shook his head, not wishing to acknowledge that he had a personal reason for his anger. 'I cannot think it acceptable that you practised such a deception.'

'I would suggest—' her voice had turned to ice and somehow he liked her all the more for it '—that, as Duke of Amscott, it is perhaps difficult for you to understand the realities of life for women or less privileged men. Lady Maria had a very good reason for not wishing to attend the ball, and, had she not gone at all, people would have asked questions. Because she is a woman. I did not wish to become a governess, but I have no alternative. I do enjoy parties; that was the only ball I will ever have had the opportunity to attend as a guest. Because I am poor. When you have experienced being either a woman or poverty-stricken or both, I shall accept your criticism.'

James frowned. 'I do of course have the advantages of birth, wealth and sex, and I am sorry that you have had no alternative but to accept a role that you do not want.' They should not have practised their deception, however. Although…her words about being poor and having no further opportunity to attend a ball were very sad. She had seemed to enjoy the dancing very much.

He still didn't know who she was, other than Lady Derwent's goddaughter, or how she came to be in this position.

'You are a lady,' he stated.

She inclined her head.

'May I ask your name and why you came to be a governess?'

'I am sorry but I can see no reason to prolong our acquaintance. I wish you very well, and I apologise for any distress I caused you with the deception.' She gave him a quick smile—a small one, not one of her wide, joyful, wonderful ones—and then turned and hurried in the direction of the maid and her charges, calling to them as she went, so that if James attempted to speak to her again he would cause a scene.

He couldn't do that to her, of course, so he just stood, impotent, hands on hips, watching her walk away from him, wondering what he would do next.

He had the strangest sense that if his life were a play, everything up to the evening he'd met her had been the first act.

And now he'd entered a different stage of life, one in which this lady—whose name he still did not know—might, perhaps, feature heavily.

She couldn't, though. She had deceived him and she was a governess.

He should probably stop being so fanciful and put her out of his mind.

The nameless lady—*she*—was now surrounded by her charges, whose smiles and laughs, their faces upturned to hers, suggested that they were very fond of her.

The little group disappeared around a corner, and James felt, well, bereft.

Maybe he should go after her after all. Find out her name and direction, request further conversation with her.

He took a couple of steps in the direction of the path they had taken, before checking himself. He should not cause the lady any difficulties with her employer unless he was going to propose marriage to her.

This morning, he had been certain that he would propose to her.

Now, however, he really wasn't sure. Well, of course he wasn't. All he knew about her was that she was a governess who had pretended to be Lady Maria Swanley and had spent an evening dancing and conversing with him.

He was definitely not going to propose to her.

He had had a lucky escape.

Chapter Five

Anna

Anna felt as though her legs would barely hold her up as she shepherded the children and Elsie around the corner.

What a horrible coincidence that the duke had come upon them like that. She came here every morning with the girls and rarely saw persons of quality out exercising. It was the wrong time of day for them—too late for gentlemen's morning gallops, and several hours earlier than the fashionable hour for the *ton* to be seen driving in the park—and it was also not the fashionable part of the park.

It had been extremely unlucky.

And extremely…upsetting.

She had spent a lot of time since the ball thinking about the duke and their evening together. When she'd told him that it had been the best evening of her life, she had not been exaggerating. It had been truly wonderful. Their dancing and their kiss had been truly perfect. But the thing that had been the best of all had been their conversation. She had felt as though they had had a genuine connection. And then, afterwards, she had wondered whether she had imagined it; she had thought that the duke probably met and forged connections with women all the time.

And then she had discovered from Lady Maria and her godmother that he had been to call on her the day after the ball. Her godmother had told her that he had at the very least wished to pursue his acquaintance with her, given his tenacity in asking about her.

It was hard not to wonder whether he might even have proposed to her.

And whether she would have liked to have accepted such a proposal.

She wasn't sure.

He had occupied much of her thoughts and dreams since she'd met him. She had replayed various parts of the evening they'd spent together over and over in her mind.

But men were not to be trusted.

Her mother had brought her up as a lady. When Anna's father had left, they had moved to a well-appointed, medium-sized house in a Cotswold village, living as a respectable widow and her daughter. They had socialised with the local gentry and had attended assemblies in Cheltenham. Anna had had every expectation of continuing to live in such a way. And then her mother had become ill and Anna had spent a lot of money—all their money—on doctors. And then, after her mother had died, she had discovered that she was entirely penniless. Lady Derwent had taken her in and had asked her, many times, to live with her as a companion, as the daughter she had never had. But Anna could not bear to take charity, and had decided that she must earn her living.

And here she was.

Of course the duke would never propose to her now.

And that was probably—certainly—for the best. Because she would never wish to be trapped in an unhappy marriage, and she knew that men's affection and love for their wives—and daughters—could fade.

Although she would have liked to have had children. But she must not dwell on these things.

She should be grateful for her employment and her friends and not think about the duke or about her life before her mother had become ill.

The way to avoid thinking about things was to keep her mind occupied in other ways. It was reasonably easy during the day, because looking after children made one very busy; it was the evenings that were more difficult.

Her employers, Sir Laurence and Lady Puntney, were very kind people.

Lady Puntney had told Anna that she did not wish her to be worked to the bone and that she must have early afternoons, evenings and regular days off, and enjoy excursions with any friends she might have.

Which was very kind, but it did mean that Anna had a good deal of spare time.

Sir Laurence had generously told her that she might read any of the books in his extensive library, and she had been doing her best to distract herself with literature. Unfortunately, his tastes, or those of his forebears who had stocked the library, tended towards the stuffier sort of fiction, and what Anna needed right now was something like a modern romance to keep her fully engrossed. She was currently reading Virgil in the original Latin, and it was a struggle to maintain her concentration; she regularly found herself staring at the same page for what felt like hours on end.

She had also tried to occupy herself in writing letters to friends, in particular Lady Maria and Lady Derwent, but had found it difficult to write much. Her words had tended towards the melancholy, and she did not wish to be or sound melancholic.

And she had never been particularly gifted at needle-work.

'Anna.' Isabella, the youngest of her charges, was pulling at her arm. 'You weren't listening.'

'I'm so sorry, Isabella; I was momentarily distracted. You should nonetheless strive for greater politeness yourself. One should not pull on another's arm like that.'

That evening, when she had finished her work for the day and was about to go to the library to try to find herself a more enthralling work of fiction than Virgil, perhaps something written in English, at least, the Punt-neys' butler, Morcambe, handed her a note that had been delivered to her during the afternoon.

It was in a thick envelope and addressed in a deci-sive-looking script.

Something made her heart beat a little faster as she pulled it out, and as she read the signature, she began to feel almost faint with shock.

The note read:

Dear Miss Blake,
Would you be so kind as to accompany me for a short drive or walk when you are next able?
Yours,
James, Duke of Amscott

How had he found out who she was?

Well, that was a silly question. She realised that she had been naïve to think that she could effectively remain hidden from him.

It would have been easy for him to establish her identity in any manner of ways. Dukes had all the means in the world to undertake detective work, or of course her godmother might have decided to tell him; she had certainly been vocal about her disappointment in Anna's choice to become a governess rather than accept her charity and had begged her to remember that she could always choose to live with her, and Anna was sure that she had been trying to make a match between her and the duke. No, her godmother had promised her that she would not betray her to him, and Anna did trust her. He must have found out some other way.

Her mind was wandering; she didn't need to speculate how he'd discovered her name and where she was staying. She needed to decide what she was going to do now.

She couldn't see him. It would be too difficult and there was no point. And people might see them and talk.

However...

He seemed very determined and very tenacious.

Perhaps it would be better in fact to meet him once in person and explain definitively that she would not be meeting him again.

Maybe she would not reply immediately but instead reflect on the matter for a while.

Half an hour later, she was still in the library, having completely failed to choose a new book because all she could do was think about whether or not she should meet the duke.

She *was* going to meet him, she suddenly decided, as she picked up and discarded a book containing the poems of John Dryden. Otherwise, she would constantly wonder whether she might see him again anyway. Every time she left the house she would be distracted, looking over her shoulder, wondering whether he might be around the next corner. That would not be an enjoyable way to live; it would be better to meet him once and be done with it.

She sent off a note suggesting that they meet in three days' time—sooner than that seemed *very* soon—she felt as though she needed to prepare herself in some way—but longer than that would just be a *lot* of probably disagreeable anticipation—and within the hour received an affirmative response in his decisive script.

And so now she just had to wait and wonder. For three whole days. She should in fact have suggested tomorrow.

The day of their meeting dawned fine and fair. They had agreed to meet at two o'clock in the afternoon, a time at which the children were regularly looked after by their nursemaids while they played for half an hour after their luncheon.

Anna had already taken a small number of solitary walks in the early afternoon to visit shops to purchase necessaries and on one occasion to take a walk with Lady Maria, who had told her all about the duke's visit to her. Anna had not enjoyed hearing about his evident bewilderment, anger and perhaps misery when he'd realised that he'd been deceived, but had been powerless to stop herself asking for every detail of Lady Maria's conversation with him.

Despite her busyness with the children, the morning and luncheon passed very slowly until eventually it was time for Anna to ready herself for her walk with the duke.

Regarding herself in the looking glass, she reflected that she looked very different from how she had at the ball. Her hair was dressed in a plain manner now, pulled close against her head and fastened into a knot at the nape of her neck, and her dress was equally plain: a brown serge morning dress, which paid no particular note to the fashions of the moment.

Anna sighed, and then chastised herself mentally. She had known that this was her lot and she was extremely lucky to have found herself employment with such a pleasant family; and she had had the good fortune to enjoy that one week in London with Lady Derwent and the experience of attending the ball. There were many people in significantly worse situations than she, and she must not complain.

Five minutes later, she let herself out of the front door of the house and trod down the four wide steps leading to the pavement, before turning left towards the corner where she'd agreed that she would meet the duke.

He was already waiting for her.

He had taken her breath away when he was dressed in pristine evening dress, and he took her breath away again now clothed in plain but exquisitely tailored morning dress.

'Miss... Blake,' he said as she drew near to him.

'Your Grace.' She could hardly hear her own voice over the immense thudding in her ears from her racing heart, and all of a sudden her legs felt quite weak.

This was silly. She was just...

She was just going to go for a walk with the only man whom she had ever kissed, a man who was devastatingly attractive and to whom she had lied. Of *course* her heart was beating fast.

'Shall we walk?' He held his arm out to her and, after a little hesitation—it seemed odd for a governess to walk holding a duke's arm—she took it. 'This way?'

They turned left from Bruton Street, where the Puntneys lived, into Berkeley Square, and began to stroll along the side of the square.

A silence, which Anna did not like, began to stretch between them.

'It is a beautiful day for the time of year,' she ventured.

'Yes, we are lucky.'

They relapsed into silence for another minute or so, until the duke said, 'Could I ask... That is to say: I am aware that this is of course none of my business, but are you happy; is your employment palatable to you?'

'Certainly I am happy, thank you,' Anna said robustly. It *was* none of his business, but she had already treated him shabbily in deceiving him at the ball; she could not be rude to him now as well.

And she was *not* going to give in to the thoughts that intruded too often that the life of a governess could become very sad; she would of course have the opportunity to become involved in and shape the lives of her charges but she would be entirely at the mercy of her employers as to how long she remained with them and whether she was able to continue her acquaintance with the children when she no longer worked for the family. And as a governess she was now in a strange position, neither servant nor member of the family.

No. She should not allow herself even to think these things. She was very fortunate in her employers; they were very generous and paid her a salary of eighty pounds per year, where many governesses in their first role with a good London family might expect no more than forty pounds, and if she was careful she should be able to save most of it. And she had very good friends in Lady Derwent and Lady Maria. Indeed, Lady Maria had recently informed her that she would be appointing her godmother to her first child.

So Anna would certainly not end up in the poorhouse and she would have friends to correspond with and she was much more fortunate than many.

And she would of course become used to her new situation very soon.

'I am glad that you are happy,' he said.

'Why, thank you,' Anna said, allowing herself to sound a little acerbic. She did not require his pity.

'I apologise. Perhaps that sounded a little patronising.'

Anna *really* didn't want to be rude, whatever the provocation, and she also still, obviously, felt guilty about her masquerade at the ball, so she didn't exactly agree with him; she just murmured something that he might interpret how he liked.

He laughed. 'You're right. It did sound patronising and you are too polite to say so. What I meant was... well, yes, I would like to think that you're happy and, yes, I think I should perhaps say nothing else on the subject.' He paused, while Anna tried to hide a smile because it was really quite endearing how much he was tying himself into knots, and then he continued, 'This is another thing that is difficult to say without sounding patronising or odd but I would like to let you know that I have not asked any further questions about you other than your name and direction. I did not wish to intrude.'

'May I ask which of my friends furnished you with those details?' She could not help feeling that, if one were prone to melodrama, one might describe it as a betrayal.

'I did not ask your friends and I do not think they would have told me. I mentioned it to my man of business. He has his ways. I apologise; I should have told you that immediately so that you would not feel let down by Lady Derwent or Lady Maria.'

'Thank you!' She smiled at him; whatever else, he was very thoughtful.

There was a brief pause again, and then the duke said, 'This way perhaps?' when they came to the corner of the square, and they continued straight ahead, in the direction of Hyde Park.

'The trees are turning very autumnal,' Anna said.

'Indeed they are. The leaves are most attractive at this time of year.'

'Yes indeed.'

Anna suddenly realised that she did not wish to feel any regrets after this walk. There could be no friendship between a governess and a duke, and, even if there *could* be, it was quite possible that if the duke ever found out that her father had been a groom he would cease any acquaintance with her, so there was no point in their seeing each other again. If there was anything she would like to say to him she should say it now.

'I would like to apologise for having deceived you,' she said. She had partially apologised when they'd met in the park, but not entirely, because at the time she'd been quite angry with him. She *should* apologise, though. 'I would like to explain in more detail how it came about, if I may.'

'I should be very interested to hear in full.'

'Lady Maria and I went to the same seminary in Bath. She is my dearest friend. She is a few months younger than me. I am now two-and-twenty years old. She did not come out when she was younger because very sadly her family suffered a series of bereavements. Her parents wished her to make her come-out this year. But she, for reasons that are not mine to divulge, did not wish to do so. When her parents left town to visit Maria's grandmother, Maria's mother asked my godmother, Lady Derwent, to chaperone Maria to the various balls she was to attend. She came to take tea with Lady Derwent and me, and told us how she felt.

'It was my godmother who suggested the deception, thinking that it would be nice for me to go to a ball and that there could be no harm in it. Lady Maria thought it an excellent idea and I, despite seeing the obvious problems that might arise, such as did in fact arise, allowed myself to be carried along with the plan because I had never been to a ball in London and desired to go to one. My godmother provided me with my dress and escorted me there. I do realise that we should not have entered into the deception and I apologise for having got a little angry with you in the park.'

'No; I must apologise for my initial lack of understanding. And my own anger. And you are right that had you and I not met and…and spent time together… it might have been possible for the deception to go unnoticed, had Lady Maria not been home to callers the next day and then retired to the country.'

'That is exactly what my godmother said when she was persuading me into joining in her plan.'

'Clearly it is a case of great minds thinking alike.'

Anna laughed. 'Perhaps.'

She was very pleased to have had the opportunity to say all that she'd just said, she realised.

Clearly, frankness was a good thing.

'Why did you wish to meet me for this walk?' she asked.

'I…' The duke paused for a while, and then said, 'That is a good question. I don't really know. I think I just wanted to confirm to myself that you were happy. And find out—perhaps entirely out of curiosity, which is of course quite reprehensible—why you indulged in your masquerade. And perhaps I had some residual anger about it, which is now dissipated, because I accept that you could not have predicted how the evening would progress.'

'I see.' She did not entirely see, but of course a duke had a different life from that of most people. He probably wasn't used to not finding out the answer whenever he felt curious about something. It would be like a normal person having an itch that they couldn't reach.

'May I ask why you consented to come for the walk?'

'You may.' There could be no harm in her being honest. 'I think that had I not met you today I would have wondered if I *should* have met you, and what you wished to say to me, and I do not find it particularly comfortable constantly wondering about something.' And *that* would have been an itch that continued to irritate.

'I see. You know, I think I have just worked out why I asked if we could meet.' He paused for a moment as they entered the gates of the park. 'I feel that it is possible that even by the end of my sentence I will regret saying this to you, but I think that I wished to see you again because I…missed you.'

'Oh!' Anna felt her heart give the most enormous lurch.

'Yes, *oh*. I think I was right in predicting that I would regret my words. May I change the subject and draw your attention to that particularly assiduous woodpecker there?'

'Certainly you may. I have always liked the green of a woodpecker's beak.'

'Green is a delightful colour.' A laugh entered the duke's voice as he continued, 'I believe that I have already mentioned that I very much like the green of your eyes.'

'It is very kind in you to say so, and also something that a duke should not be saying to a governess,' said Anna repressively. She really did not wish him to flirt with her now. When she had been playing the role of Lady Maria, that had been one thing, but now, well, now she needed to maintain her reputation and she did not wish to be beguiled into thinking in *that* kind of way about the duke.

'I must apologise,' said the duke instantly. 'You are quite right.'

Anna did not wish any further awkward silences to arise between them. It was clear that this should be their last meeting, and from his immediate agreement with her words it was obvious that he agreed. She knew how much she could enjoy his company, and she might as well make the most of it now, for these last few minutes.

'We could perhaps take a turn around this small pond,' she said, 'and then I will need to return. I will be instructing my charges on geography this afternoon.'

'Indeed? Which geography will you be teaching them today?'

'I found an atlas with a particular emphasis on the British Isles in my employer's library, and whilst, being girls, they might not have the opportunity to travel further afield than England, I hope that they might be able when older to travel to other parts of this country, so I plan to instruct them most carefully in the geography of England.'

'I agree that a knowledge of geography is a very important part of a good education. Have you travelled yourself?' asked the duke.

'I know Gloucestershire well, as I grew up there, as well as Bath and Somerset, where my seminary was and where Lady Maria's family home is. I have never, however, travelled to the north of England. I believe the Lake District amongst other areas to include wonderful scenery that I should like to have the opportunity to visit one day, but of course I don't know whether that will happen. It is something to aspire to for the future. Have you travelled, Your Grace?'

'Yes, I was fortunate enough to do a Grand Tour when I was younger, and have also had the good fortune to travel within England.' He stopped, and then said, 'I am aware that I have been very lucky to have the opportunity to travel; I'm not sure that I recognised that sufficiently at the time.'

'I hope you don't feel that you must almost apologise to me for your fortune in that regard,' Anna told him. 'It is not your fault that you were born to the life you lead, any more than it is a chimney sweep's fault that he was not.'

'That is true, but it is difficult at times not to feel the weight of good fortune.'

'That is of course to your credit, but, rather than apologise to me, tell me some of your most interesting stories. I love to hear first-person accounts of such travels rather than reading about them in fusty books.'

'Well now, that is quite a challenge. I feel beholden to tell you some stories that are either genuinely amusing or genuinely interesting or genuinely not common knowledge.'

'Yes, indeed.' Anna found herself twinkling up at him as they walked slowly along beside the pond. 'I shall certainly be judging you most severely on the quality of your anecdotes.'

'How many anecdotes would you like?'

'Hmm.' Anna pretended to consider. 'Since you have raised the categories yourself, I should like one amusing, one interesting and one not common knowledge.'

The duke nodded very seriously. 'I accept your challenge. Let me prepare for it first.' He squared his shoulders and then rolled them, which made Anna giggle.

And then he told her some truly *excellent* stories, which took them most of the way back to the Puntneys' house and made Anna wish greatly that she could walk with him again.

When she had finished laughing at the conclusion to a story about how he had mistakenly stumbled into a literary salon, when under the impression—due to his imperfect grasp of the Italian language—that he would be attending a masquerade and was therefore dressed as a monk, they were at the end of the Puntneys' road.

'You have succeeded very well in the challenge,' she told the duke, trying very hard not to feel low at the thought that she might well never see him again. 'I am most impressed.'

'I feel a little guilty that I have monopolised the conversation since we were at the pond.'

'Not at all; I very much encouraged you to tell me your stories and I very much enjoyed them. For example, I have never had another first-hand account of someone meeting an elephant and do not think I shall do so again.'

'In that case I shall say that I am pleased to be of service.' The duke stopped walking, and Anna did too, because she was still holding his arm, very much as though their arms belonged perfectly together, which was clearly a silly thing to be thinking. 'I am not pleased, however, that you have not had the opportunity to tell me any of *your* stories; I should very much enjoy hearing anything you might say, getting to know you better.'

His words made Anna feel both very warm inside and very sad that there would be no opportunity for them to talk further. She took her arm away from his because there was no need to hold it when they weren't actually walking, and she was a little worried that she might start to cling on to him if she didn't move away a little.

'It is very kind of you to say so,' she said in as hearty a voice as she could muster, to avoid any of the emotion she felt surfacing, 'but I am sure that I have nothing of interest to say.'

'Firstly—' the duke turned a little so that they were facing each other under the tree beneath which they were standing '—everything you say must be of interest to me, and secondly I cannot believe that you do not have interesting stories. Looking after young children must give rise to many anecdotes. Who is the naughtiest of them?'

'Lydia, the youngest, is particularly naughty,' Anna owned, 'but in the most adorable way. It is in no way a character defect—' she was already extremely fond of all the girls '—but merely liveliness. But it does give rise to some quite extraordinary situations at times.' And then, as they continued to stand there under the tree, she found herself telling him about the slugs that Lydia had smuggled into her mother's bedchamber and the ensuing screams when they had been discovered by Lady Puntney and her maid.

'Oh, my goodness,' she suddenly said across the duke's laughter, which was truly the most attractive laugh—deep and rumbly—that she'd ever heard; she was sure that one could listen to it every day and not get bored. Clouds had crossed the sun and caused the sky to grow much darker. 'Do you know what time it is? I must hasten back.'

'Of course,' the duke said immediately. 'I must apologise for keeping you.'

He held out his arm to her and she took it wordlessly

and they began to walk along the road towards the house at a very fast pace.

'I very much enjoyed the walk; thank you,' the duke said when they reached the house. 'May I have the pleasure of walking with you again?'

'Oh, no, I'm not sure…' Anna was suddenly a little breathless. 'I thought… I'm not sure that we should make a habit of this. I don't think that it is usual for a duke and a governess to walk together.'

'Perhaps just one more walk, so that we might finish our conversation?'

'Is it indeed unfinished, though?'

'I believe that it is.' Anna knew that she had to be firm, even though it felt so—stupidly—deeply sad to say goodbye now. It could not benefit either of them to spend more time together. And, even if she were someone whom a duke might marry, would she want to place all her dependence on one man with whom she had already, she had to admit, felt such passion? Knowing the way her grandfather and father were capable of treating women, could she trust any man? If ever she were to have the occasion to marry, would it not be better—safer—for her husband to be someone whom she liked but did not feel great passion for?

'Perhaps one more walk? In due course? If you like?'

'I don't know.' She was very tempted but really she shouldn't. She looked up at the house; she didn't want anyone to see her with the duke. 'I must go inside now; goodbye.'

'Of course.' He immediately let go of her arm, which instantly made her feel a little bereft. Truly, she was ridiculous. 'Goodbye. I hope to see you again.'

'Goodbye.' Anna decided not to reply to his last few words; she didn't trust herself not to be weak and say perhaps they might meet again.

She purposely didn't look back at him as she went through the door, and then, as she closed it behind herself, regretted not having allowed herself one more look at him.

It would definitely be for the best not to see him again.

Chapter Six

James

James was disappointed that Miss Blake didn't turn for one last goodbye as she entered the house, and then he was disappointed in himself for being such a fool.

Bruton Street, where she now lived, gave directly onto Berkeley Square; it was astonishing to think that the entire time he had been wondering about her whereabouts she had been living so close by. As he walked the short distance in the direction of his home, he found himself scuffing at leaves with his foot, dissatisfied with…well, life. And himself.

Was Miss Blake right, that dukes and governesses should not go for walks? Would he be compromising her? He wouldn't be compromising her in terms of her eligibility for marriage in that he didn't know of a single bachelor of his acquaintance who would look amongst the ranks of governesses for a wife. Would he, though, be compromising her in the eyes of her employers? Would she be in danger of losing her job if she were seen with him regularly?

Maybe. If so, he should of course not see her again. Perhaps, though, it would not matter.

He did not, he realised as he kicked a particularly large pile of leaves, have any idea what Society's rules were for governesses, beyond being aware that they occupied quite a unique space in the social hierarchy. They were ladies, and certainly not servants. But they were working for a living and could not therefore be regarded as part of Society.

Why did he care? Why was he interested? Did he really wish to see her again? Was he still tempted to propose marriage to her?

Did dukes marry governesses? Could *he* marry a governess?

What was her birth? It must be respectable, presumably. Lady Derwent was her godmother and she had been educated at the same Bath seminary as Lady Maria.

Why was she a governess?

And had he not decided last week that he had had a lucky escape because he didn't *want* to fall in love with the lady who would become his bride, and hadn't it occurred to him that he could be in danger of falling in love with her?

So would it perhaps be better if he did not pursue their acquaintance any further?

He rounded the corner of the square. More leaves. He gave those a kick too.

Maybe he would ask her if she would like to take just one more walk.

Not immediately, though. It would be poor behaviour to make her feel under any kind of obligation or pressure to meet him again.

* * *

When he walked into the main drawing room in his house, very ready to bury himself in the newspapers for some time, to give himself some respite from thinking too much about Miss Blake, he found his mother and two of his sisters in the room.

'James.' His mother beckoned him over to her. 'We should decide on the date of your wedding.'

'We should? But I have not yet decided on a bride. And I have not yet ascertained whether any young lady would consent to marry me.' He didn't sit down because he clearly wasn't going to want this conversation to continue for any length of time; he would much rather go to his study to look through some papers there.

His mother frowned and indicated very forcefully with her eyes and raised brow that he should sit beside her.

'I thought we had agreed that you were on the point of proposing,' she said.

'It is a very big decision. I need time to feel certain that I am making the right one.'

'I do understand that.' His mother's tone had softened. 'But equally I do feel that time is perhaps of the essence.'

From his side, James could understand his mother's impatience. She had lost her husband and two oldest sons in the space of only two years and was obviously still grieving, and much more anxious generally than she might have been before, and she had her five youngest daughters to think about. The oldest of his sisters was four-and-twenty and had been married for four years and had two daughters of her own now. His next oldest sister was only seventeen and not coming out until next year—his mother, while eager to know that her children were provided for, did not approve of marriage for young ladies before the age of eighteen. And his four youngest sisters were two sets of twins of fourteen and twelve.

That was a lot of people to ensure security for.

'Yes,' he said. She was right. Time was of the essence. He did need a son as soon as possible. What if the same illness that had struck his father and brothers struck him?

He wished he'd never met Miss Blake. She was confusing him too much. He needed to be able to think clearly.

Three days later, James had boxed hard at Gentleman Jackson's Boxing Saloon, he had ridden hard, he had boxed again—Gentleman Jackson had asked him if it was anger that was causing him to spar so well and James had just boxed even harder—he had played cards with friends and drunk far too much the evening before last, and he had attended two balls and the opera once, and he was still struggling not to think about Miss Blake. But he was now, with his mother, standing outside a house on Clarges Street, about to pay a call on Lady Catherine Rainsford, who remained his mother's preferred candidate for his hand.

'Perhaps after today you will feel inspired to make an offer,' his mother said to him just as the door was opened by the Rainsford family's butler.

'Perhaps,' said James unenthusiastically.

Within fifteen minutes, as he and Lady Catherine sat and smiled at each other and occasionally produced a few insipid words before smiling some more, he knew

104 When Cinderella Met the Duke

that he couldn't do it. So many little snippets of sentences or references reminded him of Miss Blake, or made him wonder what her views on them might be, or caused him to imagine her laughing when he responded with sarcasm or wonder what joke she might make. It was as though he was under a spell, and he could not in good conscience propose to one woman while temporarily in thrall to another.

He intended to be an unfashionably faithful husband, as his own father had been, and, while he did not want to fall in love, he did not want to be thinking about another woman throughout his marriage.

What he should probably do was see Miss Blake again, if she were willing, and have a long conversation with her, get to know her better, and see if that put paid to this inconvenient hankering after her company that he was currently feeling. It felt like an infatuation; he needed to cure himself of it before committing to marriage with someone else. And everyone knew that familiarity bred contempt; if he spent more time with Miss Blake, he would no doubt cease to be so curious about her.

Three hours later he was waiting with bated breath for a response to the note he had dashed off asking Miss Blake if she would care to accompany him to Gunter's Tea Shop to sample their ices. Four hours later he was still waiting. And by the time he left the house for a dinner with close friends at White's, he still felt on tenterhooks even though it was clear that he was not going to receive a reply this evening—or, perhaps, at all.

There was still no reply by the time he took luncheon the next day.

And then, late in the afternoon, he received a note addressed in Miss Blake's hand. Even her handwriting appealed to him, he realised, as he tore open the envelope. It was well-formed, easily legible, very attractive to look at… Reminiscent of the lady herself in many ways.

If her handwriting appealed to him, the content of her note did not.

> *Your Grace,*
> *I regret exceedingly that I am unable to meet you again.*
> *Yours sincerely,*
> *Anna Blake*

And that was obviously that. Clearly, he could not beg her, or make her feel uncomfortable, by asking again. He could, of course, hover regularly in Bruton Street or go to Hyde Park when she would presumably be walking with her charges, but that would be shocking behaviour when she had told him so definitively that she did not wish to see him again. That really was very much that.

And everything suddenly felt very flat.

He didn't particularly want to do anything now, but he was not going to allow himself to sink into any kind of misery just because a young lady—a governess— had told him that she did not wish to accompany him to a tea shop.

He had managed to keep his own spirits and those of his mother and sisters reasonably steady through the terrible loss of his father and brothers, so he was certainly not going to succumb to despondency over Miss Blake.

She was just a lady with whom he had enjoyed a very pleasurable evening and a nice walk.

And now he was going to go into the library and look through the post that he had received earlier in the day and had not opened because he had been waiting for Miss Blake's note.

The usual invitations and various other missives he had received caused him to sigh with boredom, but he continued. Soon, this feeling would pass and he would carry on with his life perfectly happily, and by the end of the Season he would, he trusted, have come to an agreement with a pleasant and suitable young lady.

He was almost yawning as he pulled out yet another note, written in an ornate script. He'd begun to make little bets to himself as to what each invitation would be. This one he would wager would be a dowager's musical soirée.

It was in fact an invitation to call with Lady Derwent in two days' time.

He re-read it. Yes, it was indeed addressed to him rather than to his mother.

Well.

It seemed very likely that the invitation was related to his acquaintance with Miss Blake. And therefore of course he was going to go.

When he arrived very punctually—at the somewhat surprising time of half past two—to see Lady Derwent, her butler showed him immediately towards the same saloon in which he had been on his previous visit.

As he approached the room, he heard more than one female voice from within. And…if he wasn't mistaken, one of them was Miss Blake's. Or was that just wishful thinking? He had thought he'd caught a glimpse of her more than once in the park and in the street and had whipped his head round each time only to discover that he'd been wrong; this was probably just the same.

The butler opened the door for him and announced his name.

And if James wasn't mistaken, there was an audible gasp from within.

And, yes, as the door opened wider, he saw Miss Blake, sitting directly opposite, her beautiful mouth formed into an O shape and her eyes wide.

She remained like that for a long moment, before recovering her composure and casting her eyes down, whilst murmuring, 'Good afternoon, Your Grace.'

'You are early,' Lady Derwent admonished him. 'I had not expected you for another hour.'

James looked at the clock on the mantelpiece and frowned. He could not directly contradict her but he *knew* that he was exactly on time.

And then he looked at her more closely. He couldn't say exactly in what way, but he could swear that she looked almost sly at this moment. As though she were plotting something.

Had she planned this on purpose? Invited him at the same time as Miss Blake so that they would meet each other again?

He looked back to Miss Blake. She was now sitting with her hands folded in her lap, her eyes downcast but otherwise looking entirely composed.

'I do apologise,' he said to Lady Derwent. 'I must have misread your writing.'

'Or perhaps misremembered,' she said. 'Well, no matter. Now that you are here, you must take tea with us. I shall ring for Buxton.'

'I must take my leave,' Miss Blake said.

'Nonsense,' Lady Derwent told her. 'You have only just arrived, and I still need to hear your news and tell you mine. The duke will not mind. None of us need to pretend that you have not already met.'

'No, indeed,' agreed James. 'I think we are all aware that we met at the ball.'

A tiny gasp came from Miss Blake's direction.

James was tempted to ask her if she was quite all right but decided that it would be better to ignore the sound.

'Your news, Anna,' Lady Derwent said. 'You were telling me about your excursion to the British Museum. I am sure His Grace would be interested to hear about it.'

'I am afraid that I have little of interest to tell,' Miss Blake—Anna—said. 'As we were on the point of looking at the Rosetta Stone, Lydia declared herself quite ill, and we had to leave very quickly.'

'Was she genuinely ill or just not very interested in historical artefacts?' James asked.

'The latter, I fear. I considered reprimanding her and then decided that a far better punishment would be to take her very seriously and insist that she keep to her room for the remainder of the day and take just some chicken broth. She was extremely bored and recovered remarkably quickly.'

'You are clearly an excellent governess,' Lady Derwent said approvingly, while James smiled. 'I should not like to think of your allowing the girls to be naughty.'

James raised one eyebrow very slightly at Lady Derwent. Surely this was the pot calling a kettle black; pretending to be ill to avoid being bored at a museum could not compare with instigating an impersonation of a ball guest.

'I know what you are thinking.' Lady Derwent leaned forward and rapped him over the knuckles, which James saw out of the corner of his eye caused Miss Blake's eyes to dance. 'Irrespective of what they might do in later life, it is important for children to be taught to behave properly.'

'Indeed it is,' Miss Blake agreed. 'And I am doing my best to instil discipline into them. It is hard sometimes, because one is tempted to laugh.'

'Did you have a governess, my lady?' James asked Lady Derwent very blandly.

'I did, and she failed utterly to indoctrinate me with discipline, but that is not to say that other children should not be taught better than I.'

Miss Blake laughed. James adored her laugh. It was light but full, and, if you caused that laugh you felt very proud of yourself, and if you did not know the reason for her mirth you immediately wished to find out the reason for it.

And now he was laughing at himself for thinking far too much about *her* laugh.

'Were you educated at home or at school, Your Grace?' Miss Blake's question was the first of a personal nature that she had asked him; he had had the impression that she did not wish to discuss either his life history or her own. Perhaps she felt on safer ground with Lady Derwent present.

'I began with nurses at home in the country, and then had a succession of tutors—some did not stay long because my two older brothers and I were close in age and not well disciplined, and then I went to Eton, followed by Oxford.' He looked at Miss Blake. He would very much like to know more about her background. 'I understand that you were educated in Bath, at the same establishment as Lady Maria?'

'Yes, I was, and we both enjoyed it there most of the time.'

'Were you both angelic students?' he asked.

'Not always,' Miss Blake admitted. 'But I flatter myself that my experience of breaking the rules a little will make me a wiser governess.'

'I think you're right,' James agreed. 'In fact, one might say that you were particularly prescient in undertaking any naughtiness. You were merely exploring all options for the future.'

'Exactly.'

'Did you ever swap identities with someone?' he asked.

'I must reprimand you, Your Grace, for such a particularly indelicate question.' Miss Blake tsked. 'We do not refer to specific past misdemeanours.'

James laughed out loud. 'Apparently I must apologise.' He realised that at some point he had clearly entirely forgiven Miss Blake for her deception at the ball.

'Indeed you must,' Miss Blake told him.

'Were you instructed at home before you entered the seminary?' he asked, still very interested to hear all about her early life.

'Her mother, my dear friend, instructed her,' Lady Derwent said. 'Your Grace, are you a devotee of poetry? Before you came, we were discussing Lord Byron's *The Bride of Abydos.*' It was very much as though she was changing the subject. Did she not wish him to discuss Miss Blake's childhood with her?

'I must own that I do not regularly read verse,' he said, and the conversation continued from there, through literature—with minimal contribution from James—and a discussion of the library of Miss Blake's employer and James's own library.

'Sir Laurence's library is remarkably well-stocked,' Miss Blake concluded.

'Does he have copies of the romances you like so much?' asked Lady Derwent.

'Sir Laurence does not share my taste in that regard, for which one can only admire him.'

'I, however, *do* share your taste.' James could not believe his luck. This would give him a very good excuse to see Miss Blake again. 'That is to say, my mother does, and she would very much like to lend her books to you, I know.'

He would have to remember to purchase the necessary books. He could enquire of his married sister perhaps which would be the best ones to buy. Or perhaps he would just buy all such books stocked in London so that there could be no possibility of his disappointing Miss Blake.

'Oh, no, I couldn't possibly.' Miss Blake shook her head firmly.

'Nonsense.' Lady Derwent sounded even firmer. 'I think it a marvellous idea. You are working very hard, my dear, and you will be a better governess to your charges if you enjoy your reading when you are resting. His Grace will, I am sure, bring the books to you when you next have a spare moment. Perhaps tomorrow? Or the day after tomorrow?'

'Thank you.' Miss Blake spoke a little faintly—Lady Derwent was indeed very forceful—and James would almost have felt sorry for her if he had not been so pleased that he would have such a good opportunity to see her again. 'That is extremely kind. Perhaps if you…you could perhaps send a footman with them?'

'I am sure His Grace will be very happy to deliver them to you himself. In fact…' Lady Derwent looked thoughtful.

James had the strongest sense that he and Miss Blake were pawns in some game that Lady Derwent was playing. Did he mind? He wasn't sure. It would of course depend on whether the aim of her game aligned with his own. At this point he wasn't entirely sure of his own aims. He did want to see Miss Blake alone again, for the purposes of curing himself of this ridiculous infatuation. And then he would like to marry someone with whom he would not be desperately in love. It did not seem particularly likely that that was what Lady Derwent was planning.

'I'm afraid I must leave now.' Miss Blake gathered her gloves and reticule and rose to her feet before her godmother could continue down whatever line of thought she had begun. 'Thank you so much; I have very much enjoyed our tea.'

Lady Derwent rose too. 'I would usually suggest that His Grace escort you home, but as he is so recently arrived I should like to talk to him for a few moments. One of my footmen will walk with you.'

James also rose, in order to bid Miss Blake goodbye. As he took her hand in his and looked down into her beautiful green eyes, he found it an effort not to press her fingers far more tightly than a mere goodbye warranted.

'I will look out for those books for you on my return home,' he told her.

'Thank you; that is very kind.'

And then she was gone and the door was closed behind her, and Lady Derwent was gesturing him to be seated.

'Now.' She leaned forward and tapped him on the knee. 'I believe that my goddaughter's reluctance to prolong her acquaintance with you comes from a belief that a governess cannot have a friendship with a duke. Of course, one would imagine that it might be quite irregular. But it would not be irregular for a duke to propose to a governess who was a gentlewoman of good family. It *would* of course be irregular for a duke to pursue a friendship with a lady whom he did not wish to marry.'

'Yes.' He would have liked to have asked what Miss Blake's birth was, but did not, he realised, have quite the same knack for outrageous frankness that Lady Derwent had.

'I expect my goddaughter to be treated well, as you would treat any other gently born lady,' Lady Derwent said.

'I would never wish to do her any harm,' James told her.

'Then I imagine that you will make up your mind one way or the other as to what you want as soon as possible. In the meantime, I shall be holding a literary salon on Friday. Given your interest in modern literature, you will be pleased to attend.'

'Thank you.' Good God. James very much hoped that Miss Blake would also be made to attend, otherwise it would almost certainly be a torturous experience. *Could* governesses venture out in the evenings? Did they? He really did not know. He would just have to hope.

'And now, I find myself a little fatigued,' Lady Derwent told him. 'I look forward to seeing you on Friday.'

James laughed. It didn't surprise him that his mother and Lady Derwent did not like each other. They were so similar that they could be nothing but bosom friends or sworn enemies.

The next afternoon, at two o'clock, after a very busy morning visiting first his astonished sister—she had not seen him before luncheon for several years—to ask about the latest popular novels, and then Hatchard's bookshop on Piccadilly, James was outside the Puntneys' mansion, looking forward to seeing Miss Blake.

As he lifted the knocker, though, he suddenly realised that he couldn't do this. She had been cajoled, effectively, into seeing him, by her godmother and by him.

If she did not wish to see him then he should certainly not force her to do so.

It was pure selfishness in him to wish to see her, spend time with her, in order to cure himself of the infatuation he currently felt. He had felt that there was a mutual attraction between them. What if she had felt it too, and what if she were disappointed if he asked her to accompany him for a walk and then did not wish to see her again?

He should not do that.

So when the Puntneys' butler opened the door to him, he asked him if he would be able to present the books to Miss Blake with his compliments on behalf of Lady Derwent, before handing the pile to him and leaving.

He would just have to hope that time would help him forget his ridiculous infatuation.

Chapter Seven

Anna

Anna had been—pathetically, she knew—unable to help herself peeking out of the window at the street below to see whether the duke would indeed come to see her with the books.

She had known that she would be very grateful to have them, if he did come.

She hadn't been sure whether or not she would be grateful to see the duke himself, though.

If she was honest, she *loved* his company, but it could be of no benefit to her to see him again, and so she would prefer to put an immediate end to their acquaintance.

And yet…when she'd seen him round the corner into the street and walk along with what looked like four books under his arm, her heart had given the most tremendous lurch.

When he disappeared out of sight after going up the steps from the pavement to the front door, she couldn't help going over to the looking glass above the mantelpiece to pat her hair into place, and then allowing herself to give her cheeks just the tiniest of pinches to bring a little colour to them. She smiled at her reflection and almost danced to the door to begin to descend the stairs from her attic floor in anticipation of being told that she had a caller.

She was in the hall before a footman had reached her and...

Oh.

There was a pile of books on the marble-topped chiffonier to her left, with a card on top of the pile, and no sign of the duke.

She felt her smile drop and her hand go to her throat. She'd been so silly. *So* silly.

The duke had obviously *not* been intending to see her or as interested in her company as she was in his. He had obviously just been *made* by her godmother to provide the books and had been too polite to demur. So he had clearly dutifully collected some together and had brought them and...gone away again.

And that was *perfect*, she thought, as she looked at his card. *Perfect*. Exactly what she would have chosen, in fact. Definitely.

Three days later, at eight o'clock in the evening, she alit from Lady Puntney's carriage outside her godmother's house. Truly, Lady Puntney was the most wonderful employer; she had told Anna that she positively *insisted* that she attend Lady Derwent's literary salon because it could only benefit the girls if their governess discussed literature with people who knew the great Lord Byron well. She had also whispered to Anna, in a joking fashion, poking fun at herself—because, as she had already owned, she was hoping to climb as high in Society as possible, in as nice a way as possible—that if Anna wished to introduce her to such an illustrious personage as Lady Derwent, that would be wonderful.

Truly, there was no need to hanker after the friendship of the duke. Anna was most lucky in both her employer and her godmother, not to mention her wonderful best friend, Lady Maria, who would be here this evening.

Lady Derwent had told Anna that the evening would comprise a select group of ladies meeting to discuss the most recent work of Jane Austen, *Emma*.

Most fortuitously, *Emma* was one of the books that the duke had delivered to Anna on Tuesday, and from the first page she had loved it. She had read late into the night, until her candle burnt out, for the three nights since she had received it, unable to put it down. She had finished it that afternoon, while her charges rested with their nurses, in lieu of taking her usual afternoon walk around the garden square. Forgoing her daily exercise was in direct contradiction of her own strict tenets on how a lady should live, but it had been worth it because she had very much enjoyed the ending of the story and would now be in a position to discuss it with the other ladies.

Lady Maria greeted her at the door to the salon with her arms held out, and Anna embraced her gladly. Her godmother then hurried over.

'Anna, dearest.' She pulled her properly into the room, and said, 'Allow me to introduce you to our fellow devotees of literature.'

As Anna was introduced to a series of ladies, she was

extremely grateful for the dresses with which her god-mother had presented her before she took up her governess role; the one she was wearing now was a delightful primrose yellow muslin, which she knew was of the latest mode and hoped became her quite well. Everyone here was smartly attired and she would not have enjoyed wearing one of her brown or dark blue day dresses.

'I'm delighted to…' She suddenly gave the most tremendous start in the middle of greeting a very well-dressed lady of perhaps forty years old whom Lady Derwent had introduced as a Mrs Travers; she had perceived out of the corner of her eye, at the far end of the room, a group of three men.

Two of them were dressed rather unusually, the way one might imagine poets to dress, with loose jackets and spotted cravats. And the other…

The other was a tall and broad gentleman with thick dark hair and very neatly fitting and not at all poetic-looking clothing, and an expression of slight horror on his face, which made Anna's lips twitch, even as she felt her stomach churn.

She forced her attention back to the ladies to whom she was being introduced, and flattered herself that she managed to produce quite acceptable smiles and greetings, despite the whirring of thoughts inside her head.

And then her godmother took her over to the men.

She introduced Anna to both the spotted cravat wearers, while Anna tried very hard to focus on the introductions and produce a few polite words, while her mind whirred and her eyes seemed to want to swivel in the direction of the third gentleman.

And then Lady Derwent said, 'And, of course, you

are acquainted with His Grace,' and Anna was able to look directly at him without appearing rude.

Anna and the duke said, 'Indeed,' at the same time. He inclined his head slightly, his expression unmoving, and she gave him a small smile.

'Thank you so much for the books.' Anna had of course written a note thanking the duke—a note that had taken her far more time than it should have done to compose—but obviously must thank him properly now.

'It was my great pleasure. I hope that you will enjoy them.'

'I have already finished reading *Emma* and enjoyed it exceedingly; I am sure that I will enjoy the others too, and am very grateful for the opportunity to read them. I must confess that I was so engrossed in the story that I read late into the night three evenings running and was only stopped by my candle burning right down; I am very eager to start the next one but will wait a little, both to enjoy the anticipation of it and to recover from the lack of sleep that I experienced this week.'

The duke laughed, and said, 'I'm very pleased to hear how much you enjoyed it and will be equally pleased to lend you more books from my mother's collection when you have finished those. Which do you intend to read next?'

Anna's reply—Fanny Burney's *Evelina*—was interrupted by Lady Derwent clapping and addressing the assembled company.

'We are now going to discuss Jane Austen's *Emma*. For those who have not read it but intend to do so, those of us who *have* read it will take great care to avoid telling you what happens at the end. Let us arrange ourselves so that we can converse more easily as a group.'

Within a small number of minutes, with a firm and slightly terrifying authority that Anna imagined many army generals could only dream of attaining, Lady Derwent had directed the assembled company to sit in a semicircle.

Somehow—Anna was sure that it was by design but had not been able to pinpoint how she had actually managed it—Lady Derwent contrived to seat the duke on the left-hand end of the half-circle, with Anna immediately to his right, so that if he wished to enjoy any quiet conversation it could only be with her.

Truly, her godmother was incorrigible in her apparent quest to throw Anna together with him.

And truly, Anna's heart should not be lifting in the way that it was at the prospect of more time talking to him. Allowing herself to enjoy his company could only lead to despondency in the future. Clearly nothing could come of an acquaintance between them; dukes did not marry the daughters of scandal, and indeed that was a good thing: Anna should keep on reminding herself that she had seen the misery caused by her parents' incompatibility—both in rank and in temperament—and did not wish to participate in such a union herself. Husbands in general were rarely to be relied upon.

Having finished her directions, Lady Derwent seated herself in a large chair that had been placed facing the middle of the semicircle, and some distance back so that she was able to see everyone without having to turn her head too much.

'With whom should we commence?' She looked in the

duke's direction, very much as though she had always intended to ask him first. 'Amscott, as one of the few gentlemen here, should you like to give us your thoughts on the main themes of the book?'

'I…am…still reading it and so would not like to say too much now in case my views change when I reach the end of the book. Which I am very much enjoying.'

'What did you think of Emma herself at the beginning? And of Mr Knightley of course?' asked Anna, unable to help herself poking a little fun at him. It was extremely obvious that he had not read any of the book at all.

'I thought Miss Austen's execution of the entire book was masterful. I like her use of literary devices and the setting in which she places the story and her characters. I should be very interested to hear your views on her writing, not to mention her characterisation. Of Emma and Mr Knightley in particular,' the duke replied. Quite masterfully, in fact. He really did give the impression of almost knowing what he was talking about.

'One last question,' Anna said, really unable to resist. 'What did you think of the relationship between Jane Fairfax and Frank Churchill?'

The duke narrowed his eyes at her for a moment, which made her lips twitch further, before smiling blandly and saying, 'I very much enjoyed reading about their relationship. I thought that it was written very well. I should very much like to hear your thoughts now, though. I fear that I have been monopolising the conversation for too long.'

'I would be very happy to—perhaps—bore you with

my many thoughts, as I quite devoured the book, but have one final question for you,' she said.

The duke nodded and murmured, 'Of course you do.'

'Who was your favourite character, and why?'

The duke shook his head. 'No,' he stated. 'I enjoyed the book so much that I cannot choose. I do not mean to imply that I found each character equally worthy of my liking or equally flawed, but they were so well drawn by the author that I cannot choose one above the other.' His head was turned in the direction of Lady Derwent, but he shot a triumphant glance in Anna's direction as he finished speaking, which caused her to have to swallow a giggle.

'Most illuminating,' Lady Derwent said. 'Anna, do you agree with the duke's thoughts?'

Looking straight back at her godmother, trying hard not to be very conscious of the duke's eyes on her, Anna said, 'They were certainly very comprehensive. More specifically...'

She had a lot to say, having read the book so very recently and having enjoyed it so very much, and soon was so engrossed in conversation with others who had genuinely read it that she almost at times forgot how close to the duke she was sitting and how if she moved a little to her left their shoulders and thighs might almost brush against each other.

It was wonderful. She hadn't previously experienced discussing literature with others in this way; her parents had not been readers, and Lady Maria and her other friends at the seminary had been reluctant scholars at best—although it did seem this evening as though Lady Maria had read at least some of *Emma*. Perhaps the problem had been the dry nature of their reading material at the seminary.

The discussion—with nods and murmured agreement from the duke—continued for a gratifyingly long time, with, amongst other things, different opinions offered as to Miss Austen's motivation behind her writing, the reasons that the writing was so particularly effective, and discussion as to whether any of her characters might be based on people whom Miss Austen knew, and whether any of the present company might have met any of those people.

As the conversation eventually descended into general gossip, Anna found herself turning to the duke—it would have been rude of her not to have done so as he would have had no one else with whom to converse—and being unable to resist the temptation to say, 'You must be pleased not to be dressed as a monk this evening.'

He cracked a laugh. 'I am delighted not to be dressed as a monk and even more delighted that my telling you that story clearly made an impression.'

'I must confess I would have enjoyed seeing you in religious garb this evening.' She smiled at him and added sarcastically, 'You look as though you are *very* pleased to be here.'

'As you will have noticed, I am extremely devoted to all forms of literature and very much in my element here,' he said, rolling his eyes just a little, which made Anna laugh.

'I do hope that hearing our thoughts will not have ruined the end of the book for you, Your Grace,' she said with faux sincerity. 'I understood you to say that you had read most of it already, and certainly your expressed thoughts indicated a wide knowledge of the book.'

'What I was most proud of in the expression of my thoughts,' he replied, 'was that they were so very applicable to almost any well-written work of fiction. And of course one's views on any book one has read are subjective, and so I could not be called wrong.'

Anna laughed. 'Very cunning; I am not surprised that you feel proud. Are there any books that you have read recently that you would like to discuss in more specific detail?'

The duke narrowed his eyes at her. 'Without wishing to be impolite in any way, I cannot answer that question until I understand the possible consequences. Would I be required to discuss the book more widely, and is there a risk that I would have to do so today?'

'My godmother wrote to me yesterday to ask if there was a particular book that I should like to discuss at this salon, and I understood from her that our conversation would be confined to the works of Jane Austen, but I'm sure that if you wished to hold forth about another author we should all be most eager to hear what you had to say. I would be very happy to suggest that to my godmother.'

'I cannot believe you would treat me so shabbily after I sent you the book that you have just enjoyed so much.'

'You are quite right.' Anna gave him a fake contrite smile. 'I am very grateful and must no longer torment you.'

'Indeed you must not.' His smile, coupled with the way he was gazing into her eyes as though the rest of the company did not exist, was suddenly making her feel quite breathless.

'If I give you my assurance that I will not mention your answer to anyone else,' Anna said, trying hard not to be too overcome at his proximity, the intimacy of his lowered and beautifully deep and raspy voice and the squareness of his jaw, 'would you tell me your favourite author?'

The duke leaned another inch or so closer to her. 'If it is to remain our secret—' the increased raspiness of his voice caused Anna's skin to raise in goose bumps '—I am prepared to confide in you.'

'I shall be honoured,' she said, still breathless, 'to be the holder of your confidence.'

The duke's eyes dropped from her eyes to her mouth for a moment, and Anna swallowed.

'That is…good to hear,' he said.

Anna found herself moistening her lips with her tongue.

'So…my secret.' He was looking at her lips again, and Anna felt as though they were the only two people in the world.

'Mmm?' she breathed.

'You must remember that you have promised not to tell another soul.'

'I shall remain faithful to that promise.' She could not have told why this conversation felt so extremely daring.

'So your question was…? I just want to make sure I answer it quite correctly.' The duke turned a little further in her direction, his eyes not moving from her face, and the sides of their knees brushed.

'Oh,' Anna squeaked.

A small smile played about the duke's lips and Anna smiled back.

They were just *looking* now, gazing at each other, as though they were quite alone.

Which they were not, she suddenly remembered.

'The question,' she said, as firmly as she could.

'Ah yes, your question. *Any* question, Miss Blake, and I will answer it as long as my response remains secret.'

Anna took a deep breath. Her stomach seemed to have turned completely liquid. A very warm liquid.

What had they been talking about? What *was* her question? Oh, yes.

'Who,' she breathed, 'is your favourite author?'

'My favourite author,' the duke said very slowly, and Anna could not help watching his beautifully firm mouth as he formed the words, 'is—' he leaned even closer to her and their knees brushed even more '—Jethro Tull.'

'Jethro Tull?' Her voice had gone squeaky again.

'The only author I have read recently.'

'I am not—' she was almost forgetting what they were talking about, because the way he was gazing at her was so—well—*exciting* '—familiar with Mr Tull's works.'

'He wrote about agricultural machinery and farming methods in the last century. I have just been dipping into his work *Horse-hoeing Husbandry.*'

'Oh. How…fascinating.'

'Extremely fascinating.' The duke's lips quirked up and Anna couldn't find any more words, because it didn't feel as though it was just Mr Tull whom the duke found fascinating.

And then they just sat and smiled at each other, and Anna felt as though her heart might beat right out of her chest.

She loved the tiny lines at the corners of the duke's

eyes when they creased as his smile grew, as it was doing now, and she loved the sheer breadth of his shoulders and the way she could see his muscles move under his tight-fitting jacket. And she loved just *being* with him.

He was looking at her lips again and she wondered whether she might explode. She really did need to restart some sensible conversation.

'How often do you read Jethro Tull? And how many books did he write?' she asked, trying not to sigh at the sheer deliciousness of this conversation.

'I am not sure exactly how many books he wrote and I am not an avid reader but I do on occasion enjoy reading—' the duke's voice dropped a little '—when I am in bed, before I go to sleep.' His throat worked as she stared at him, unable to stop herself imagining him in, well, *bed*. The way he was swallowing indicated that perhaps he was having similar thoughts. Perhaps in relation to her.

'In bed,' she repeated, and then gasped. What was she *saying*? Respectable governesses did not talk about *beds* with unmarried men. Especially not in a literary salon in the company of others.

She took a very deep breath and said, 'I must try Mr Tull's works myself,' with as much briskness as she could muster.

'I would be very happy to lend them to you any time you should like to read them.' The duke's tone was very serious, but his eyes were very playful, and the combination was irresistible.

'I should not like to deprive you of your own reading matter,' Anna replied, only just capable of forming a rational sentence.

'My feeling…'

To Anna's huge disappointment, the duke was interrupted by Lady Derwent clapping her hands. 'I think it's time that we all took some refreshment.'

She had groups of small tables surrounded by chairs at the other end of the salon, and they all dutifully followed her over to them.

'I would like to sit with my goddaughter and of course the duke,' she announced. 'I make no pretence that I don't enjoy the company of a handsome young man.'

And before Anna had time to think about whether she was pleased or not to be seated at the same table as the duke and her godmother, she'd been marched by Lady Derwent over to her table.

'I must say, Amscott—' Lady Derwent took a dainty bite of a small crab tart '—your blathering about the book was admirable. One might almost have imagined that you had read it.'

The duke leaned back in his chair, his broad shoulders far too wide for its back, and grinned. 'I was not aware until four days ago that you were summoning me to this salon. Had I had longer, I would of course have been delighted to have read the entire book.'

'In that case—' Lady Derwent smiled triumphantly '—I shall tell you now what book we intend to discuss next time.'

Anna felt herself smiling inside at the thought that there would be a *next time*, even as she realised that it would be very dangerous to allow herself to become too attached to such occasions.

Perhaps, though, perhaps she might have an interesting and full life if she could continue to attend select events like this with her godmother. And perhaps one day she might meet a man whom she could hope to marry who might make her feel the way the duke made her feel. Actually, why had she just thought that? Hadn't she decided that if she could avoid it she would not like to be married? Or if she did marry should her husband not be someone who did *not* make her feel the way the duke did?

'Next time?' queried the duke, and Anna immediately felt her spirits sink a little. Which was very silly; this salon would have been hugely enjoyable even without the Duke's presence, she was sure.

'Next time,' her godmother said firmly.

The duke laughed. 'I will of course be more than happy to attend—' he glanced for the merest of seconds in Anna's direction, which made her smile '—any number of book discussions.'

'Do you undertake to produce an equally profound analysis of any book, Your Grace?' Anna asked with her most demure air.

'Certainly,' he said.

And then he nudged her foot very gently under the table with his own foot, while continuing to hold a particularly bland expression on his face, which made her gasp considerably less gently.

'Are you quite well, Anna?' her godmother asked.

'Very well, thank you.' Which was true as long as her heart didn't jump right out of her body with all the thudding it was doing as she wondered what the duke might do next.

The three of them then conversed amicably on a number of unexceptionable topics, and the duke behaved equally unexceptionably throughout. Which was really quite disappointing.

When in due course some of the guests began to take their leave, Anna stood up too, with some reluctance.

'Thank you so much for the evening,' she said to her godmother. 'I have enjoyed it exceedingly.'

'You will go home in one of my carriages,' Lady Derwent instructed. 'The duke will escort you outside.'

'Of course.' The duke stood up very promptly and held his arm out to Anna, and to her shame she felt herself almost wriggling with internal delight to have another opportunity to touch him, even in a completely innocent way.

As they descended the steps outside the front door, he leaned down so that no one around might hear, and said, 'We were interrupted in the middle of a conversation earlier. Perhaps we should resume it. Would you care after all to visit Gunter's with me? I believe the ices there are the best in London.'

Anna knew that she'd thought about this and decided that it was not a good idea to see the duke alone—or at all—again, but right now she couldn't remember why she'd thought so, and it also seemed that there could be little point in not accompanying him there if she was, for example, going to see him again at another literary evening.

So she said, 'Oh, well if they are the best in *London*, perhaps I cannot refuse.'

'Excellent.' His smile melted Anna's insides. 'I shall look forward to it. I will write to you tomorrow to arrange the time.'

As he handed her into the carriage, the duke pressed

her hand just a little more than was necessary, in the most delicious way, almost as though he were promising something, and held her gaze for far longer than necessary as he smiled at her.

Anna smiled back at him, wordlessly, and knew that she would look forward to their visit to Gunter's far more than she ought.

Chapter Eight

James

James had made hay while the sun shone and had written to Anna immediately on waking the next day to arrange to visit the ice cream parlour.

The response had taken far too long for his liking; it had not arrived until the afternoon. It was an excellent response, though: Anna had agreed to go to Gunter's with him the next day.

He drew up on Bruton Street in his curricle at the time they had agreed, feeling far more excited than any grown man should at the prospect of going to a tea shop and eating ices.

He needed to remind himself that the reason for spending a little more time with her was to confirm that they would not in fact be compatible as life partners. He just needed to cure himself of his ridiculous infatuation.

As he lifted the knocker on the Puntneys' front door, he reflected that he could no longer think of Anna as Miss Blake after hearing Lady Derwent address her by her Christian name. The name Anna was perfect for her: classic, poised, elegant, lovely-sounding and with a little cheekiness to it. Good God. It seemed as though the literary evening might have had an effect on him; he had become quite poetic.

The Puntneys' butler asked him to wait in the hall for a moment and rang a bell. Shortly afterwards, he heard steps and Anna came into sight around the bend in the staircase.

She smiled when she saw him and James smiled too and all of a sudden it was as though his day had brightened. And there was that damned poeticism again.

'Good afternoon,' he said, more interesting speech having deserted him for the time being while he got used to the very pleasant fact that he was with Anna again. 'You look very nice today. As always.'

She laughed. 'Thank you.'

She was wearing a dark green velvet pelisse over a dress of the same colour, with a cream beading. She looked delightful, and also expensively dressed. She couldn't possibly have the means to buy herself such clothes on a governess's salary, and indeed when he had seen her in the park she had been wearing a much less fashionable and intricately tailored gown. She had obviously fallen on hard times to have chosen to become a governess. How, he wondered, did she afford her clothes? Perhaps they were from her previous life. Or a gift from someone, perhaps Lady Derwent.

He would like very much to know how it had happened that she had become a governess. He did not like to think of her being in need.

'It is a beautiful day,' he observed, as they descended the steps outside the house.

'It is indeed,' Anna agreed. 'I had feared that it would continue to rain but the clouds seem to have entirely disappeared now.'

'Were you able to take your charges out this morning for their walk between rain showers?'

'We did manage a short one and I think that their nurse will take them into the garden for an hour now.'

'Let me help you up into the curricle. I have a blanket for you to wrap around your legs to keep you warm.' It was very pleasant taking her weight on his arm for a moment as he handed her up, and really quite disappointing that she had already arranged the blanket entirely successfully by herself before he was seated next to her and could offer to help with it.

'Thank you,' she said. 'I have not been in a curricle before; this is the most wonderful treat.'

'I am pleased that it is.' He took the reins and nudged his horses to start walking. 'Do you…' James very much wanted to ask her more about her background. Was he being curious for the sake of curiosity? No, he realised; he had begun to care about her and wanted to know whether she was genuinely happy. 'How did you come to be a governess?' Asking leading questions could only seem patronising; it was surely better to ask directly. Although…she might not wish to tell him. 'I'm sorry; please don't feel that you have to answer that question.'

'I am happy to answer it,' she said after a short pause. 'I think mine is not an unusual situation. My parents were sadly somewhat impecunious, and while my mother was alive we had enough money, but with her loss I also lost all financial means. I realised that I would have to earn some money, and was extremely fortunate to find this position with the help of Lady Derwent. She would have very happily paid me to be her companion, but she is not yet at the stage of life where she genuinely requires one, and I would prefer to maintain our relationship as it is, without receiving too much charity.'

'I'm so sorry about the loss of your parents. Was it recent?'

'Thank you. My father, he, that is to say, I… We…' She paused and then continued, 'We lost him some years ago. My mother more recently. I am very lucky in having such a wonderful godmother, however. I know that you have also experienced loss; it is deeply tragic but I believe those of us who have the good fortune still to be here must do our best to enjoy the life that we have, when we are ready, of course, after the first deep grief.'

'I agree.' He took the reins in one hand and covered her hand for a moment with his own. What he wanted to do, he realised with a shock, was hug her tightly against him to comfort her if he possibly could.

'Thank you. And that is why,' she said, a slight tremor in her voice indicating perhaps that she felt more emotion than she was owning to, 'we must enjoy every last morsel of our ices today.'

James laughed. 'I agree with that too.'

As they drove at a leisurely pace down the road and into Berkeley Square, where Gunter's was located, part of him just enjoyed being physically in her presence, part of him produced vague small talk to match hers, and part of him reflected on what she'd just said. He realised that she had answered his question about her background without answering it in the slightest. What was the story behind any lady of quality becoming a governess? Any such lady would have been brought up in the way Anna clearly had, and would then have fallen on hard times and decided that she needed to seek employment.

And while she had confided in him the information about the loss of her parents, of *course* she had lost them; she would presumably not otherwise have to work as a governess.

Her answer had in fact been very similar to his about Miss Austen's book: quite generic.

Of course, she had answered in that way because she didn't want to give him any further details, whereas the reason that he'd answered in that way had been that he hadn't read the book. He should respect her wish not to disclose more. And since he was only here to cure himself of the ridiculous infatuation he felt for her, there was no need for him to find out anything else about her background.

'On a different note,' he said, 'but continuing with the theme of making the most of life, I was so taken by your passion for *Emma* that I have started reading it myself. I don't think many amongst my friends have read it and presume that Miss Austen might have had a female audience in mind when she wrote it, but I must own that I am enjoying it and that I do, like you, very much like the way she writes, and her wit.'

'Well! I am very pleased to have been of service to you. And I have to admit that I am a little surprised. On Friday you did not have the air of a man who wished to engage closely with literature.' Anna glanced sideways up at him as she spoke, with a smile that held a cheeky edge, and James smiled back at her.

And then they had one of the moments that they'd been having where they just smiled—foolishly—at each other without speaking.

James had slowed the horses to a standstill outside the tea shop. Anna's face was tilted up towards his, and he had a feeling that if they were not in quite such a public space, he would not be able to help himself doing what he'd done at the ball, and leaning down and kissing her. *Damn*, he wished he could. Her lips were slightly parted, her cheeks were a little flushed, her sea-green eyes were framed by long eyelashes, her gaze was direct, and the whole made for, well, for extreme temptation.

They were, however, surrounded by other stationary carriages; it was common practice for people to drive up and be served as they waited.

'A waiter will come soon to take our order,' he told Anna, to distract himself from the lushness of her lips.

'I am very much looking forward to tasting the ices.' She frowned. 'How are you reading *Emma* having given your copy of it to me?' she asked.

Damn. He was an idiot. If he wasn't careful, he'd end up admitting that he'd bought all the books he'd 'lent' to her. He had in fact bought a second copy of *Emma*.

'My sister and mother both had copies of it. You can never have too many copies of a good book.' He was an excellent liar, it seemed. He wasn't sure whether he should be proud of that or not.

'Oh, I see. Thank you again for lending the books to me. I am of course able to give them back to you any time you desire.'

'I would be very happy for you to keep them for as long as you like. From what you have said, I believe you to be a much keener reader than any in my family other than perhaps one or two of my sisters, and I'm sure that every author would like his or her books to be read as widely as possible.'

'Thank you.' The smile she gave him would have been more than enough reward for something considerably greater than the procurement of a few books.

'My very great pleasure, I assure you,' he told her.

'Tell me about your sisters? It sounds as though you have several?'

'Well.' James was more than happy to talk about his family, whose company he liked very much. 'You must interrupt me immediately if I talk for too long. There is a lot to say: I have six sisters.'

'My goodness.'

'Indeed.'

He had her laughing with several anecdotes about his sisters, which he found immensely gratifying. He liked the sound of her laugh, and he liked to think that he had made her happy in some way, and everyone enjoyed laughing.

As he watched a waiter approach them, he finished another story about his two youngest sisters, and said, 'I have been speaking for far too long. Do you have any siblings?'

'No, I don't. I would have liked to, I believe. It must be wonderful to be surrounded by so much family. Oh, look at the different ices that people are eating.' She nodded at the occupants of some of the other carriages. 'I have no idea what flavour I'm going to choose.'

She clearly did not wish to talk about her family for long. Perhaps it was understandable given her recent losses. And of course he certainly should not lead the conversation in directions she did not wish to follow.

'There are certainly some quite remarkable flavours,' he said. And then he added, 'I have been here a few times before, always with my sisters,' because for some reason he did not wish her to think that he'd escorted any other young lady here in the way that he'd escorted her.

A few minutes later, as Anna perused the menu, he took the opportunity to watch her. Her face was beautifully expressive and the colour of her hair quite delightful. He could happily just look at her for a long time. Which, frankly, seemed a little odd, as though he'd lost his wits.

'My goodness,' Anna interrupted his thoughts, looking up from the menu. 'I know that you've been here before but I can't resist reading some of these flavours out loud; some of them seem quite remarkable. We may choose between maple, bergamot, pineapple, pistachio, jasmine, white coffee, chocolate, vanilla, elderflower, Parmesan, lavender, artichoke, and coriander.'

James could not recall a time when he had more enjoyed someone reading a list. He very much liked Anna's voice, and he very much liked the way she wrinkled her nose at him when she found something amusing.

'By what are you most tempted?' he asked.

'I can't quite decide. I should like to taste the ones that I think will be *nice*, obviously, but I should also like to taste the ones that I think will be *odd*. Just to see what they're like. So I fear that I am going to be most indecisive.'

'May I make a suggestion?'

'Of course.'

'Why don't you choose several ices—some odd and some nice—and taste them all?'

'I don't like to waste anything,' she said. 'One sees and hears of such poverty. It does not seem right to order food that one knows one cannot finish.'

James wondered what poverty she had experienced herself to have decided that she needed to work.

Her point was valid and he did not wish to waste food either, but he did want her to have a good time and to taste whatever she wanted.

'I have an idea,' he said, pleased with his own genius. 'Choose a small selection now and we will return soon and taste more of the flavours. I am very happy to return as many times as you like.'

'You are very kind,' she told him, smiling.

That *smile*. James was almost sighing just at the sight of it.

'I am not kind, I am quite selfish,' he told her. 'I very much enjoy your company and therefore I am heartily enjoying our visit. I would enjoy a second and indeed third or as many as you like.'

'I cannot trespass upon your kindness to that extent, but I am certainly looking forward to tasting the ices now.'

James was *definitely* going to want to persuade her to return, he thought, but he could pursue that later. Perhaps when she had tasted some of the ices and was feeling wistful about the ones she had not sampled.

'For the time being,' he said, 'I feel that you have a big decision to make. We can certainly manage four flavours between us; I am a very competent eater. Which will you choose?'

After much deliberation, during which James could not take his eyes off her as she read the menu, tilting her head to one side to think, she announced, 'I think I am quite decided. Parmesan. Obviously.'

'Obviously. You have to have a cheese one.'

'Yes indeed. Also artichoke, because I have to have a vegetable. Violet, because I have to have a flower. And pineapple and maple because I have to have one that I think I will actually like.'

'The perfect combination. Parmesan, artichoke, violet, pineapple and maple. I can't imagine a more delectable mouthful.'

'Your Grace.' She fixed him with a stern look. 'Are you trying to put me off? Because I must tell you that you are succeeding quite well and I might have to reconsider my choices.'

'Miss Blake.' He wished so much that he could call her Anna. This formality seemed ridiculous. 'Firstly, I should like it very much if you called me James.'

'Do you not think that is perhaps too familiar?'

He lowered his voice so that there could be no possibility of anyone else hearing and said, 'I do not wish to be indelicate, but I feel that when one has kissed someone, it cannot be thought improper to call them by their Christian name.'

'Oh!' Her squeak was one of the most adorable things he'd ever heard. 'Your Grace. *James.*'

'Yes?'

'You are quite outrageous.'

'I cannot apologise, unfortunately, because I enjoyed it very much.'

'I really do need one of my godmother's fans to give you a well-deserved rap.'

'My knuckles are very grateful that you do not have one. Although… I think you would look delightful peeking over the top of a fan.' He could not resist teasing her; the combination of her laugh and her pout was one of the most alluring things he'd ever seen.

'I feel that our conversation is going sadly awry. I believe that you had something else you wished to say to me?'

'Yes, I think I did.' James smiled at her. 'I think I've forgotten, though. You make me forget myself.'

Anna leaned towards him and very deliberately did a large and most unladylike roll of her eyes.

'Miss Blake. I am shocked.'

'So am I,' she said sunnily, which made James laugh, a lot.

Soon Anna joined in with the laughing, and it turned out that there was little he would rather do than laugh about absolutely nothing with this wonderful woman.

They eventually calmed down, and as they wiped their eyes, Anna still hiccuping slightly with giggles, it occurred to him that he really hadn't done very well at pushing this infatuation out of his mind.

He hadn't actually spent that much time with her yet, though. Maybe the way she ate her ices would give him pause for thought. Or maybe the way *he* ate ices would cause *her* to wish herself anywhere but here. Maybe by the end of this afternoon, they would both be heartily relieved never to see the other at close quarters again.

A waiter interrupted his thoughts to place their ices in front of them, so he was going to find out sooner rather than later whether ice-eating made any difference to his silly infatuation.

'I intend to be scientific about this,' said Anna, clearly not as distracted as he was. 'I think I'm going to start with the one I think I will like least and finish with the one I expect to like the most.'

James shook his head. 'Is that not very risky? What if the one you think you will like the least is in fact the one you like the most? It would be disappointing to begin well and finish badly.'

'That is very true.' Anna paused, her spoon mid-air. 'I need to think about this carefully.'

'But not too carefully in case the ices melt.'

'Very true. Perhaps I should take one mouthful of each in the order I expect to like them going from worst to best, and then re-evaluate the situation.'

'Very sensible,' James approved.

'However—' her spoon was still in the air '—I now realise that I am being very rude to you. Very self-centred. Which ones would *you* like to try first?'

'No, no, this is your treat and we agreed that I am just here to finish up whatever you do not wish to eat.'

'Are you sure, though? I feel that I am imposing on you.'

'You could never impose on me,' James said, very seriously, meaning it.

Anna looked at him for a long moment, her own face very serious all of a sudden, and then said, 'You are a very kind man.'

'Really, no,' he said. God. He was in fact only here

because he wished to clear his mind of the infatuation he felt for her. That was not kind at all.

'We must agree to differ and we must begin to eat or as you say they will melt.' She looked between them. 'I am of course going to try the artichoke one first, because I do not expect to like it as much as the others.'

'Of course.'

She placed her spoon in the artichoke ice and scooped a little out.

And so far, watching her take ice cream was not helping James's infatuation level at all. The way she held her spoon, the way she concentrated and then looked up at him with a little smile, were all quite delightful. Delicate but not *too* delicate.

And then she opened her beautiful mouth and put the spoon in and, oh, good God, the way she held the spoon in her mouth for a second; James was imagining her holding *other* things in her mouth. And the way she was tasting it, savouring it.

How had he managed to sit opposite her and eat an entire meal with her during the supper at the ball without exploding with desire?

As she finished the mouthful, Anna gave a little wriggle, which caused her chest to move far too alluringly for James's sanity, and said, 'I was mistaken.'

'You were?' James managed to ask.

'Yes. Artichoke ice cream is divine. You must try some immediately.'

'Certainly.' His voice sounded somewhat like a croak.

He put his own spoon into the ice and then put it into his mouth, incredibly conscious the entire time of Anna's eyes on his hands and mouth.

'That is wonderful.' He wasn't certain whether he was referring to the ice or to the way it felt having Anna's eyes following his every movement.

She swallowed and raised her eyes to his. 'Yes.'

Their eyes held for a long time, before Anna pulled hers away with what looked like an effort and said, 'We should try the next one.'

'We should.'

'Violet,' she said decisively.

And then she took a spoonful of it, and, even though he'd already seen her place a spoon in her mouth and suck gently, the sight of her doing it still caused his body to respond most uncomfortably. At this rate, he was going to be a gibbering wreck by the end of the afternoon.

Anna closed her eyes for a second and put her head to one side, looking as though she was focusing very much on the taste she was experiencing, and then opened her eyes and swallowed.

James took a deep breath and shook his head slightly to clear it.

'How was that one?' he asked, very impressed at how normal his voice sounded.

'Very nice but not as truly wonderful as artichoke. Which is the opposite of what you would expect.'

'That *is* interesting.' James plunged his own spoon into the ice, trying hard not to think crude thoughts about plunging other things into places, and tasted. 'You're right,' he said. And then for some reason he couldn't resist adding, 'It seems that we have *very* compatible taste in ices.'

'I think,' said Anna, placing her spoon very deliberately into the next ice, 'that that remains to be seen. For all we know, we might disagree enormously on the next ones.'

'That is a very fair point,' James acknowledged, as he watched her again before taking his own mouthful.

As they continued to taste the ices together, James's enjoyment of watching Anna only grew, if that were possible.

'The artichoke is still my favourite,' concluded Anna after their final tasting. 'Although the pineapple and maple is a close second.'

'I agree.' James would agree with absolutely anything she might say right now. 'And that proves that we are compatible when it comes to ices.'

'No, it proves we are compatible when it comes to *these four* ices.'

'In that case,' he said triumphantly—although he wasn't even sure that this what he wanted; he knew that at the beginning of the afternoon it hadn't been entirely—'we will have to come again and sample another four.'

'You might be right. Not definitely right, but probably. Now, I am afraid, with great regret, that I ought to return to the house.'

'Of course.' James was conscious of huge disappointment, which was at odds with what he'd intended from this afternoon. He thought. It was actually quite difficult to remember.

Maybe because his infatuation was, if he was honest with himself, growing. And maybe that was because, once Anna had told him the bald facts about her family, they'd just reverted to engaging in frivolous small talk. And so, really, he still knew hardly anything about her.

As he collected up his reins and encouraged his horses to move forward, he found himself asking, 'Do you drive?'

'No; I have never had the opportunity. I do love horses, though, and much admire this pair.'

'And of course the skill with which they are being driven.'

She laughed. 'Of *course* I admire your skill.'

James laughed too, and then found himself saying, 'I think we are fated to visit Gunter's again. We need to sample a lot more ices, as you rightly said, because we need to determine whether our ice cream tastes are indeed compatible, and I feel that you should have at least one opportunity to drive a carriage. We could combine the ice-eating with a driving lesson.'

And, good God, what had come over him? He *hated* being driven and under no circumstances—normally— would he acquiesce to a request to drive his horses, let alone *offer* such torture. He would worry about his horses and he would worry about his sanity. But now, when he thought about it, he didn't even think it would *be* torture.

Apparently he would do almost anything to spend time with Anna.

Chapter Nine

Anna

Anna did a gigantic swallow as she looked at the duke—James—holding his horse's reins and smiling at her. He was…he was…*sublime*.

His humour.

His kindness.

His strong, handsome features.

The evident strength in his arms, across his shoulders, ensured that she felt safe at all times in his presence. Well, not *entirely* safe; she was beginning to think that her *heart* might not be safe. But physically she knew he would protect her. She was *sure* he was a good driver.

She was also sure that she would be much better served to thank him for the ices and say goodbye and that she would perhaps see him another time, perhaps at another literary salon at her godmother's.

But…

'I should like that very much,' she heard herself saying.

'Why don't you take the reins now?' he suggested.

'Now?'

'Well.' He looked around at the relatively narrow road they were in. 'Not exactly now. But perhaps we could go somewhere less busy and you could begin your first lesson. I think the village of Kensington might be a good place to start.'

The sensible thing to say would of course be that she should go back now…except Lady Puntney had suggested that she take the entire afternoon to herself as she had admitted to having a headache yesterday—probably due to such a lack of sleep from reading late and then thinking about the duke—and Lady Puntney did not wish her to be ill. And so she *could* stay for just a little bit longer.

'I'd love to just for a few minutes,' she said. 'Thank you.'

'There is really no need to thank me,' he said as he manoeuvred them through what felt like an impossibly small gap and which at the hands of a less confidence-inducing driver would have caused Anna to close her eyes and cling tightly to the side of the carriage. 'Really, I'm being quite selfish; I'm sure I will enjoy teaching you.'

'In that case, I must ask you to thank me for agreeing to your suggestion.'

He smiled at her as though her very weak humour had amused him deeply, which made her smile in her turn.

They lapsed into silence, but it was a nice, comfortable one, unlike the one they'd had at the beginning of the walk they'd taken. It felt as though—even though Anna had been careful to keep their conversations quite frivolous—they had become friends.

Well, it wasn't *entirely* comfortable. Anna felt as

though her heart was bursting with…something, and she was most *un*comfortably aware that she very much wanted him to kiss her again.

When they went over a bump in the road and they were jiggled in their seats and their legs almost touched, it felt incredibly exciting and then very disappointing that they settled back into the same positions they'd been in before.

And as she watched his hands—so strong and yet light on the reins—she found herself wondering how it would feel to have them on her.

And when she looked at his profile as he concentrated on the road, and then caught his eye when he glanced briefly at her with a smile, well then her mind was filled with memories of their kiss.

'I think this is as good a place as any,' the duke said after a few moments.

'For what?' asked Anna, unable to collect her thoughts.

'For teaching you to drive?'

'Oh! Yes, of course.' She hoped he hadn't realised that her mind had been quite so far away from driving, focused at that moment on his thigh next to hers. She looked around. They were in a wide, quiet, tree-lined road, bordered by pretty houses. 'Is this Kensington?'

'Yes, it is.'

'It's very peaceful after the hustle and bustle of London. And yet really quite close.' Perhaps one day in ten or twenty years' time, when she had saved enough money from her salary, Anna might be able to purchase a small house in a place like this.

'Yes, it's very nice.' The duke smiled at her in such a way that Anna felt as though all he could see at this moment was her. It was quite intoxicating being regarded in such a way. And she feared that she might be returning his gaze with an identical one.

After a few beautifully long moments, he lifted one hand towards her, and then replaced it at his side and swallowed.

'Perhaps you should move a little more towards the middle of the seat,' he said.

Anna just stared at him, in mute question. Was he suggesting that they...

'So that we might begin the lesson,' he clarified.

Oh! Of course. Of *course* he hadn't been suggesting that they move closer so that they might kiss.

Anna nodded and slid sideways, as he did the same, until they were seated very close to each other.

Their upper arms were touching now, which was making Anna very warm inside. Apparently it wasn't making the duke's insides turn to mulch at all, though, because he was able to speak in a perfectly normal voice, saying, 'I'm going to give you the reins now and show you how to hold them. Perhaps...'

She looked up at him as he regarded her and then the horses as though he was trying to solve a particularly knotty problem.

'I must confess that I haven't ever tried to teach anyone to drive before,' he said. 'I feel that it would be prudent to make sure that I am able to stop the horses bolting if they get alarmed in any way or if you pull on their mouths, which I am *certain* you won't, but we should consider all eventualities.'

'Mmm.' Anna's heart was beginning to bang very loudly in her chest; at this rate it would be so loud that it might cause the horses to take fright. She had no space in her brain to think about holding the reins correctly because her entire being seemed to be taken up with drinking in the duke's proximity and wondering what would happen next.

'I wonder,' he said, 'whether the wisest thing might not be for us both to hold the reins, like this. If you agree.'

And he put his left arm around her so that she was encircled by his arms and held the reins in front of her. He was warm and hard and big and smelled wonderful, and Anna couldn't imagine that there could be a nicer place in the world to sit than right here, right now, within his hold.

'Is that all right?' he asked, his voice low, his breath whispering across her cheek.

'Mmm.' She really didn't have any words. She glanced over her shoulder at him and saw that he was smiling at her in such a fond manner that she almost had to close her eyes to recover from the…well, the sheer delight of it.

'So you should take the reins,' he said.

'The reins,' she repeated. All she could think about was the way her back was against his chest and just how big and hard it felt.

'Maybe we should hold them together.' His voice was low and husky and he could have said any words at all and they would have sounded delightful, exciting, fascinating…

'Mmm.'

He put both the reins in his right hand and then took her left in his—it fitted *beautifully* inside his larger hand—and transferred both reins to their left hands, and then took her right in his and transferred the right rein back.

'Look,' he said. 'You're driving.'

'Mmm.'

'You seem—' his mouth was even closer to her ear now, his breath almost tickling her '—to be unusually lacking in speech at the moment. Perhaps you are overcome by…the idea of your first driving lesson?'

Anna took a very deep breath, which caused her to be pressed more tightly against his chest, and found some words.

'That is exactly it,' she achieved. 'I am extremely overcome by…that.'

'I find you to be an excellent driver.' His voice had sunk extremely low.

'I'm not sure that I am actually driving. The horses are stationary.'

'That is a mere detail.'

'An important one, though?'

'You are demanding, Miss Blake.'

'In *every* way.' She had *no* idea where her words had come from but she had *loved* saying them. She didn't even really know what she meant by them but…

'In that case—' he tightened his arms around her a little '—perhaps you would like to move the horses on a little.'

'I think I would.'

'Go like this with the reins.' He took his hands away from hers for a moment—which she really did not like, and not just because it was a little terrifying thinking that she was the one in charge of the horses for that moment, but because she *liked* his hands on hers—and showed her what to do.

She moved the reins herself and the horses began to walk forward, in perfect harmony with each other.

'Oh, my goodness,' she said, entranced. 'They're beautiful. And I'm driving them.'

'Indeed.'

They continued to move forward in a straight line, Anna watching the proud backs and haunches of the horses and feeling the duke's embrace.

She was so deliciously happy with where she was that she almost didn't register that there was a bend coming up.

'We will need to turn,' the duke said, his mouth against her temple. 'The horses are extremely intelligent but it would nonetheless be wise to encourage them a little to follow the line of the road.'

'By pulling gently with the left rein?'

'Exactly,' the duke approved. 'You are indeed a natural driver.'

As they rounded the corner, Anna said, 'I see that it is in fact the horses who are natural drivers.'

'I did choose this pair for today knowing that they are reasonably placid, as they were going to be standing for some time while we ate,' he acknowledged, 'but I am quite certain that you would drive any horses very well with very little practice.'

They continued for a few minutes until they were beyond the village and then he said, 'Perhaps we should take this turning here.'

After a few more moments, they came to a clearing.

'I wonder whether we should stop for a moment to enjoy the scenery?' he suggested.

'I think that would be very nice.' Anna suspected that he was tempted to enjoy the scenery in the same way that they had enjoyed the rose garden at the ball. The sensible part of her mind was suggesting that it would not be a good idea to engage in any more flirting, or kissing... But the rest of her was, frankly, quite desperate to be kissed just one more time.

'We stop the horses like this,' the duke told her, helping her to apply just a little pressure with the reins.

They came to a halt under a large oak tree, still not entirely divested of its leaves despite the progression of autumn. The duke removed his arms from around Anna, leaped down and looped the reins around the tree's trunk, before returning to the seat in one lithe move.

And then he settled himself back where he had been sitting before.

'I wonder whether, without the horses and reins to distract us, we might find an even better position for you for driving,' he said, his voice very throaty. 'Like this, for example.'

He placed his hands on her waist and lifted her a little so that she was in a slightly different position against his chest.

'I think that might work particularly well.'

'Mmm.' Anna could hardly breathe. She *loved* his hands on her waist, large against her body.

'Did you enjoy that?' His mouth was almost touching her temple as he spoke.

'Enjoy…?' Enjoy his hands on her waist? Very much so, yes.

'Your first driving lesson.'

'Driving.' Of course that was what he had meant. 'Yes, thank you.'

'I enjoyed it too.' His voice was *so* deliciously throaty.

She turned a little to look up at him over her shoulder, wriggling a little against him as she did so, and smiled at him.

'Damn,' he said.

She raised her eyebrows, suddenly—even though she wasn't sure how—feeling in some way as though she was in control of this conversation. A conversation without words.

He gazed at her eyes, her mouth, her tongue as she moistened her lips.

And then she wriggled more against him and pouted a little at him.

'Damn,' he repeated.

And then, very slowly, but with very clear meaning, as though nothing could have altered his course, he leaned down and kissed her on the lips.

This kiss was different from the first one they had shared at the ball. It was not tentative, or a mere brushing of lips. It was immediately hard, and demanding, the duke's tongue entering her mouth immediately, *wanting*, wanting things from her, and causing her to want too.

She turned further towards him and reached her arms up around his neck, loving the way that the movement meant that their chests pressed against each other.

The duke groaned and then slid his right arm further around her waist.

His left hand was on her waist, his fingers on her ribs, and then it began to move up her body.

Anna took a sharp intake of breath as his hand moved to cup the underside of her breast, as all the while they continued to kiss. This felt so very, very daring, and so very, very perfect, and she just wanted him to touch her more, further…

She pushed her hands into his thick hair, almost as though she wanted to anchor him to her, as they continued to deepen their kiss. His hand was moving further now, on her breast, and *oh*. Even through the fabric of her dress, his touch felt wonderful.

And then he lifted her so that she was on his lap. He put his right hand into her hair, and tugged very gently, so that she leaned her head back a little, and then he began to kiss her very slowly along her jawline, as she sat encircled in his arms, her hands still in his hair, her body truly on fire.

With one hand he continued to caress the underside of her breasts and with the other he somehow undid the buttons of her pelisse until he had it open and was kissing her along her collarbone and then down and down, with what felt like great intent, towards the neckline of her dress.

And then, somehow—he had very clever hands— he had the neckline lower and had her breasts released from their constraints and he was kissing, caressing, nipping, and Anna was just *shuddering* with the sheer delight of it.

As he continued, she pushed her hands inside his shirt, wanting to feel his hard chest. She could feel corded muscle, and strength, and she could feel what he was doing to her, and it was utterly, utterly blissful.

As they continued to explore each other with their hands, she found herself kissing, almost biting his neck as he sucked and nipped on her, and it was one of the most wonderful things she had ever experienced.

And then…one of his hands moved to her leg, and he began to run his fingers along the length of her thigh, and even through the fabric of her dress his touch made her shiver even more, as his hand rose higher. She reached down to his thigh, marvelling at the solidity of it and the bunching of his muscles, and enjoying how as she moved her fingers higher up his thigh, his breathing became faster.

And then he moved his hand under her skirts, and now his hand was on her bare skin, tracing further and further up her leg to where she now felt liquid and… almost *desperate*.

He continued to kiss her neck, her breasts, her shoulders, tormenting and delighting, as his fingers circled closer and closer, ever higher on her thighs. She was clinging to him, one arm round his neck again now, holding his shoulders, the other on his hard thigh.

And then, finally, his fingers reached her most intimate parts, the shock of his first touch there causing her whole body to shudder.

'Your Grace,' she panted, as he began to move his fingers with what felt like real purpose. She could barely think but she knew that she wanted to feel him too.

He halted the movement of his fingers. 'I'm sorry; would you like to stop?'

'No, no, please, please carry on.'

He laughed and resumed his touch.

Anna couldn't think now, all she could do was feel, and judder and cling to him.

She reached for his breeches, feeling the hardness of him there, and worked to open them. When she had her hand on him, she felt—with great satisfaction—him judder too.

'Oh, my God, *Anna*. Call me James.'

'James,' she said on a long pant—maybe a little scream if she was honest—as his fingers began to move more and more and the pressure built.

As she spoke his name, she suddenly wondered *what* she was doing, and whether it could be dangerous for her.

'James. Stop,' she managed to say. 'Could I become with child like this?' She didn't *think* she could, but she *had* to be sure.

'Not if I do not enter you.'

His fingers and mouth had immediately stilled when she'd asked him to stop, and she didn't like it, and if it couldn't result in a baby, then she couldn't bear the thought of stopping *now*…

She didn't have the words to ask him to continue, though, so instead she just increased her hold on him and began to move her hand.

'Anna? Do you…?'

'Mmm, yes.'

'You are certain? Because maybe…' He ended on a groan as she moved her hand more.

'Extremely. Certain,' she said, moving very deliberately.

And then he moved his hand back and kissed her hard and deep on the mouth before beginning to kiss her breasts again, and then she was lost to the pressure and sensation that began to build, just on the perfect side of unbearable.

Release came for Anna, and, she realised, for James, at almost the same time.

And then they just half lay, half sat under the blanket on the carriage seat, their limbs entwined, both of them still shuddering.

Anna was the first to stir. The day had become quite gusty, it seemed from the leaves beginning to blow around them, and the breeze on her bare shoulders had made her very aware of her nakedness under the blanket. She wriggled away from him so that she could adjust her dress. *Big* adjustments were required; she was quite scandalously undressed. Well. The undress was clearly not as scandalous as what they'd just *done*. All the kissing and touching and… Her stomach was dipping just at the *thought* of it all.

'Would you like any help?' James's voice was still quite ragged, which Anna had to admit she *loved*.

'I think—' she smiled at him as she adjusted her dress across her chest '—that I might have had quite enough *help* from you today.'

He returned her smile and lifted both his hands to cup her face, and then he placed a lovely little kiss on her lips.

'I don't think I could ever have enough such *help* from you,' he said.

'James! I can't believe you just said that.'

'Really? I have a *lot* to say in response to that.' He kissed her on the lips again and then smoothed her hair back and helped her to pull her pelisse around her shoulders. 'Firstly, I love hearing my name on your lips like that.'

'Secondly,' he continued, 'you can't believe that I just made a slightly warm comment about what we just did? Because I *assure* you—' he kissed her again before tracing one finger down her chest between her breasts, which made her shiver quite delightfully '—that what we *did* was a lot more shocking than what we might say.'

His face became very serious, and then he continued, 'I must apologise if you feel uncomfortable in any way about what happened, but I assure that you cannot possibly become with child without...'

Anna shook her head. 'We had already kissed and that was quite scandalous enough already to ruin a young lady of quality such as Lady Maria. And no one knows we are here...' She knew that she should regret what they'd done, because of course it was truly shocking behaviour, and it couldn't happen again, because even an employer as kind-hearted and caring as Lady Puntney would really probably have no choice but to ask her to leave if she knew of such an indiscretion, but if she was never to be married, which seemed probable, she would at least have this memory. 'And so...' She smiled at him, to signal to him that she had no regrets, and then bit her lip, because his expression was *so* serious.

'I would never, ever want to hurt you in any way, Anna,' he said.

'I know that.' She realised that—insofar as a woman could trust a man, she did trust him very fully. Well, she trusted him fully to treat her well within the context that he had of her, which was that she was a lady who had fallen on hard times. Arguably they should not have kissed, but many people kissed, and more, before they were married, even Lady Maria and her *curate*, it seemed. She wasn't sure how he would treat her if he knew that she was the daughter of a groom. She was sure that he would still be kind to her, because she was certain that he was a very kind, honourable man, but she wasn't sure that he would wish to spend any more time with her. In her experience, even the nicest of men were bound by Society's code. 'Thank you.'

'I think I should take you back now.' He tucked the blanket around Anna and gathered the reins. 'Perhaps I will drive now, if you don't mind, for speed. We have been out for quite a long time and I should not wish Lady Puntney to comment.'

'No indeed, and yes, I will allow that your driving is a tiny bit faster than mine. For the time being. Until I have spent a few more minutes practising and have become an expert.' It felt important to try to turn the conversation entirely away from what they had just *done*.

James smiled obligingly and said, 'Of *course* you will be an expert with the reins with only a few more minutes' practice.'

They both laughed and then lapsed into silence as they began to drive back towards London.

Anna did not wish to be silent; she would not be able to avoid being alone with her remarkably confusing thoughts later on and did not wish to be free now to reflect too much on what had happened.

'It really is very autumnal now,' she observed.

'Indeed it is. I particularly like red leaves at this time of year.'

'Have you travelled to Scotland? I believe that the forests there are particularly fine?'

They passed the next few minutes in most enjoyable discussion about the different botanical and zoological features of Scotland and its islands. That is to say, at times Anna almost managed to stop incessantly replaying in her mind what she and James had *done*. Most of the time, though, if she was honest, she had only half her mind on the conversation.

Eventually, as the conversation slid somehow to the discussion of some rather scandalous *on-dits* that James had heard from his mother about some of the ladies who had been present at the literary salon evening, Anna managed to participate more fully in the conversation, and soon couldn't stop herself giggling hard at some of James's more outrageous stories.

They arrived too soon at Bruton Street, and Anna was conscious of a sense almost of loss that she would be leaving James's company so soon.

As he drew up, he said, 'I very much hope that you would like to return to Gunter's to taste more ices. We have a lot of them to experience. And also, of course, you might wish to undertake more...*practice*.' He accompanied his last word by a meaningful eyebrow raise and a *wink*, which made Anna gasp.

'James!'

'Anna! What did you think I meant? I was referring to driving. Obviously.'

'Obviously indeed,' she said, and he laughed. 'Thank you very much for a wonderful afternoon.'

'I was extremely pleased to be of service,' he said, with another eyebrow raise, causing Anna to gasp again.

'I am afraid,' she said, adopting her primmest manner, 'that I can no longer thank you *for the delicious ices* because you appear determined to make inappropriate references at every turn.'

'You are correct,' he said. 'I would like to apologise but I fear that I do not feel particularly sorry.'

Anna held her arm out as haughtily as she could. 'I feel that it is now time for me to go inside.'

'Your word is my command.'

It took a very long time for them to say goodbye to each other—without touching each other at all, because of course there might be many witnesses—until eventually Anna went inside the house.

She found it remarkably hard to concentrate on— well, *anything*—because her head was full of this afternoon with James, and, like a young miss with nothing else to think about than pretty dresses and ribbons, rather than the mature governess she was, wonder how long it might be until next she saw him.

Gratifyingly, she discovered within the space of less than two hours that James perhaps felt similarly, when she received a card in the handwriting she now recognised. The more she knew him, the more she liked his script.

She was all fingers as she fumbled to get the card out of its envelope, so keen was she to read its contents.

She found when she opened it that he had written in entirely formal language, with no reference to anything inappropriate. She was heartily relieved, because one never knew when something might fall into other hands, but also she was a little disappointed, she realised.

The import of what he had written did not disappoint, however; he wished to make an arrangement now to take her back to Gunter's to continue their ice-tasting experience. As soon as possible, he had suggested.

Anna knew that it would be very silly to repeat what they had done. She also knew that she couldn't think of anything she'd rather do.

Lady Puntney had been quite outspoken about how pleased she was for Anna to continue to see Ladies Derwent and Maria, and any other friend she might wish to meet. And it was quite unexceptionable for a lady to visit Gunter's alone with a male friend. And she would probably meet James again at her godmother's next literary soirée. It could do no harm to meet him on occasion. She was sure they wouldn't be silly enough to kiss again.

Before she could change her mind, because it really was quite tedious going back and forth with pros and cons in her mind, she dashed off an acceptance of his invitation. She would look forward to seeing him again, but just for the ices. Nothing else.

The next morning dawned grey, the clouds in the sky heavy with water. By the time breakfast was finished, the heavens had opened and Anna had to acknowledge that she would not be able to take the girls for their usual morning walk; they would get drenched if they left the house.

It was the first day since she'd begun her role as governess that they weren't able to go out at all in the morning, and it was—as she could have predicted—not particularly enjoyable; the girls steadily became less well-behaved than usual, and Anna began to feel as though the four walls of the house were closing around them.

Finally, at around half past three in the afternoon, the rain had cleared up and the sky was cloudless.

Anna, with Elsie's assistance, hurried the girls into their outer garments and boots and set off as quickly as possible, just in case the clouds were going to change their minds and return.

As she did every time she walked out of the house now, since the duke—James—had told her that he lived in Berkeley Square, which was adjacent to Bruton Street, she couldn't help wondering whether she might bump into him while she was out.

It was *impossible*, she was finding, not to think about him quite regularly when she was inside the house too.

And, as they walked into the park at this very different time of day from usual, it was impossible not to look into each of the carriages of the fashionable people that they passed, just in case she saw him…

He wasn't in any of them.

Until…there he was.

Anna almost gasped out loud at the sight of his now achingly familiar profile and broad shoulders.

Her lips began to form into a smile and then she suddenly realised that he was not alone in the carriage. He was accompanying two ladies.

One of them was his mother; Anna recognised her from the ball.

The other…was a very young and very beautiful lady, who Anna did not recognise.

Perhaps she was the duke's sister, Anna told herself.

Except…she did not resemble James or his mother at all.

And the expression of extreme politeness on James's face indicated that she was not a sibling. Anna had met enough people with siblings to be aware that they rarely behaved together as though they were only acquaintances.

James was driving with another young lady. And his mother.

Which surely could only mean one thing.

He was planning to marry the young lady.

'This way,' she told the girls and Elsie a little more sharply than she'd intended, shepherding them as quickly as she could down the first path she saw, desperate for James not to see her.

She was *so* humiliated, she thought as she sniffed back tears. And the lady should feel humiliated too, of course, because he had been doing *that* with Anna while about to become, or perhaps already, affianced to her.

Actually, she thought, staring hard at a tree trunk as though that might give her inspiration, he couldn't already be betrothed. If he were, he could hardly risk being seen at Gunter's with Anna.

Gunter's. Should she still go there again with him? She didn't know. Should she write him a vicious note saying she had seen him with someone else and both she and the other lady deserved better than that and she never wished to see him again? Although maybe she would like to say that in person. Or perhaps she should just ignore him when he arrived in Bruton Street. That would be petty, though, and she didn't want to be petty, however badly he might have behaved.

Maybe she would go with him to Gunter's, enjoy his conversation in a very dignified manner and then tell him at the end that she would not be seeing him again and that she wished him well. And perhaps she would mention that she had seen him with the other young lady. Perhaps that would be the most dignified approach, with the added benefit of telling him that she *knew*.

Yes, that was what she was going to do.

She still felt *very* low, though. Which was of course very, very silly, because she had known all along that dukes did not marry governesses. And she didn't even *want* to get married.

And, since it was silly, she was going to pull herself together and concentrate on the children.

She gave a huge sniff—rather a honking one, which caused the girls to stare at her and Elsie to ask if she was quite all right—and gave them all a big smile. The Duke of Amscott was *nothing* to her. A mere acquaintance. She was not going to let him affect her at *all*.

The next afternoon, she went shopping for paints with Lady Derwent, who had decided that she would like to produce some watercolours.

Anna decided on the way there that she would not mention *anything* about the duke.

And she stuck to her decision very well until, as they were standing deliberating in Ackermann's Emporium, she saw on the other side of the shop the young lady with whom the duke had been driving yesterday.

'Who is that?' she asked her godmother in a whisper.

'Lady Catherine Rainsford,' Lady Derwent told her, still concentrating on the picture frames between which she was choosing. And then she suddenly looked up at Anna, her eyes slightly narrowed. 'Why do you ask?'

'No reason,' Anna said airily.

'I have seen the Duke of Amscott with her a few times. I believe that his mother is perhaps promoting a match between them. I have not seen great enthusiasm from his side, however.'

'Oh, I see,' Anna murmured.

It did make more sense that spending time with Lady Catherine had not been entirely the duke's choice, but it underscored the fact that he and Anna really could not continue as friends or acquaintances or whatever they were any longer.

She would meet him one final time tomorrow. And she might as well enjoy that meeting as much as she could before she finally told him that they must no longer see each other.

Chapter Ten

James

Three days after he'd last been with Anna, five minutes before the time he'd agreed with her, James drove up Bruton Street, already smiling at the thought of seeing her again.

He'd missed her, more than it should be possible to miss someone whom you last saw less than half a week ago. He wanted to hear what she'd been doing and thinking, and he wanted to tell her countless small anecdotes about what he'd been doing, from the most mundane, like what he'd eaten, to the social events he had been to and the gossip, through to important things like decisions he was making about his estates. He would also like to ask her opinion on when his seventeen-year-old sister, Jane, should make her come-out.

She was fast becoming—had already become—someone with whom he felt that he wanted to share everything: of *course* the lovemaking, although that really ought not to happen again, but also, really, *everything* else.

He couldn't help feeling that that might not be a good thing, but he also couldn't help just wanting very much to see her.

She was ready when he arrived, dressed this time in a mid-blue, delightfully form-fitting pelisse and a jaunty-looking hat.

'Good afternoon. You are looking very well.' He took her hand and kissed her fingers.

'Thank you.' Her smile had the same effect on him that it had done each time since he had first seen it, at the ball, and he beamed at her in response.

Then he frowned. Her smile—while always beautiful—was in fact not quite so wide as usual, as though she felt some constraint.

'Are you quite all right?' he asked her.

'Yes, thank you. I…' She paused, and then looked him directly in the eye. 'Yes, I am, thank you.'

And then she walked with him to his curricle, and as he handed her up into it, she seemed completely herself again.

He realised, once he had her settled on the curricle seat with a blanket around her legs and had jumped up on his own side, that he had so many things to speak about with her that he didn't know where to begin.

He should be polite, of course, and ask in greater detail how she was.

'Very well, thank you,' she replied, 'although I am at grave risk of becoming very tired again thanks to *Evelina*, which I started two days ago and am enjoying almost as much as I enjoyed *Emma*.'

'I am very pleased that you are enjoying it, and shall read it myself when I have finished *Emma*. And I am also very pleased that you have immediately led the conversation in this direction, as I—genuinely—very much wished to enquire about your thoughts on the relationship between Emma and Mr Knightley.'

'Your Grace…'

'James?'

'James.' She twinkled at him as she spoke his name and he nearly dropped his reins. She was so very alluring. 'Am I to understand that the man who told me recently that he did not read fiction is not only reading it but *enjoying* it?'

'That is correct.' He couldn't remember the last time he had read a work of fiction, and he didn't think he'd *ever* read something quite so…*romantic*…but he was not ashamed to say that he was enjoying it greatly.

'I would like to take sole credit for your epiphany but must allow that there were many others present at the salon, so I must share it.'

'No, no, it is all you.' He smiled at her. 'I assure you that there was no other lady there who could inspire me to stay up far too late at night.'

She gasped and he said, 'Reading, I mean.'

Anna visibly swallowed and then laughed, and said, 'I am flattered, Your Grace.'

'So you should be. Every tutor I ever had, as well as my schoolmasters and dons, would be deeply impressed. And now tell me your thoughts on Emma and Mr Knightley before your head is turned by my compliments.'

'Well. How far along in the story are you? I do not wish to spoil the end for you.'

They did not stop talking about *Emma* until after they

arrived at Gunter's, when they had to break to place their order.

'I must tell you,' James said, 'that I take full credit for introducing you to these ices, in the same way that you have introduced me to Miss Austen's works, and as such I allowed myself to order a special ice for you, with a flavour combination that I hope you will like.'

'Oh, how exciting.'

'I feel that you should also choose another four to sample. In case you do not like the one that I chose. And you are certainly under no obligation to say that you like it.'

Anna laughed. 'I am sure I shall. Thank you!'

'I think that you should withhold your thanks until you have tasted it. Now, which others would you like?'

'I feel that it should be a joint decision.'

'No, no; you chose very well last time and I think we should maintain tradition.'

'In that case...'

She chose lemon, carrot, cinnamon and Gruyere cheese. When she had finished ordering, James said, 'And we would like a little artichoke ice cream as well, if possible.'

'You're very clever,' Anna said approvingly. 'We will need to compare the best of these against the artichoke so that we may find the best of all.'

'Exactly. And I am really not sure what I wish to happen: will we be sad if artichoke is removed from its position of superiority or will we be delighted to have found something even more delicious?'

Anna frowned and nodded with an air of great seriousness. 'You pose a very important philosophical question.'

James laughed and reflected yet again that he couldn't imagine a better way of spending an afternoon.

When the ices came, Anna said, 'I am quite agog to see what flavour you asked especially for.'

'Chicken and asparagus,' James said, as the waiter got them ready for them.

'Oh, those are my two favourite foods.'

'I remember from the ball. I think I remember everything you have said to me.'

'Oh!' The little squeak she gave made James smile a lot. 'Thank you!'

After a pause, she said, 'We must taste it first, at exactly the same time.'

They took their spoons, and…the taste was…odd.

'I like it excessively,' said Anna, in a most determined manner.

'I must own,' James said, 'that it is not my favourite.'

'I like it very much.' Anna took another spoonful.

'You really don't have to,' said James as she failed to hide a quite alarming wince.

'I really do like it very much—' she looked a little as though she was going to be sick '—and I am extremely grateful for the lovely gesture, but I think it would be remiss in me not to try the other flavours.'

In the end, they determined lemon to be as good a flavour as artichoke but no better, and Anna had admitted that while she was extremely grateful that he had remembered her favourite food, she would not choose to eat chicken ice cream again.

'I foresee that we will have to return here many times to determine the absolute best,' he said, as they prepared to leave. He looked over at her, smiling at him with laughter in her eyes, and wondered if it was possible that his heart had just actually turned over.

He had fully intended to drive her straight home after they had finished their ice creams, with no detour during which any lovemaking of any kind might occur. And of course, he should certainly not kiss her again, as he had no thought—well, he didn't know whether he did or not, but he probably didn't—of proposing to her. As he'd determined before, he did not wish to experience any further loss, and marrying someone he loved would of course endanger him in that way. So they ought to go straight home. But on the other side of the coin, it would be a shame for her to have no further driving practice.

'Would you like to take the reins for a short while?' he asked. 'When I have driven us somewhere a little less crowded again.'

'Oh, yes, thank you, I would.' She hesitated, and then said, 'There should be no need for us to stop along the way, though, I think.'

Which was of course ideal. It really was. Really.

Her driving was genuinely impressive and he allowed her to take the reins by herself for a while—she was a very fast learner—and James genuinely did not intend that they stop along the way…

But somehow, when she handed the reins back to him, and their hands brushed, and she smiled up at him in *that* way, he was unable to resist the temptation just to give her the tiniest of kisses, and she responded in a way that he had not entirely expected but did very much appreciate. And then it would have been, well, really quite impolite, had he not secured the reins so that he could kiss her for just a little longer, and then it seemed that neither of them wished to stop kissing. And more.

And this time it was even better than before, because this time, while they were still exploring each other, they also already knew a little about what the other liked. James realised that a man could happily spend a lifetime making Anna shudder and moan in just that way.

When they finally finished, and he was trying to help her tame her markedly dishevelled locks and adjust her clothing to an acceptable state, all he could do was smile.

'You are very, very beautiful,' he murmured in her ear as he smoothed her pelisse into place over her extremely well-formed breasts and she shivered again under his touch.

He was beginning to think that he might have fallen in love.

Did he *want* to be in love?

On the way back into London, he managed to lead quite naturally, he hoped, into a question he very much wanted to ask. 'Tell me more about your parents?' It felt odd that, though they now had a very strong connection and he knew so much about her tastes in ices, literature, travel ambitions and stripy food, he knew absolutely nothing about her background.

'They were… I'm not sure how to describe them. That is not a question that I've been asked very often. Or ever, perhaps. Since I…lost them, no one has asked.'

And she had not answered the question in the slightest. Would it be rude of him to ask again?

'I'd very much like to hear if you would like to tell

me.' He would not repeat the question if she brushed him off this time.

'My father was…hard to describe. I remember him laughing with his friends. My mother was very kind and enjoyed helping others.' And that was that. She sounded very final; she clearly did not wish to say any more.

James realised that he didn't wish to know just about their personalities. He also wanted to know *who* they were, how they had spent their lives. He wasn't sure whether he *ought* to want to know those things: did they really matter or was it enough that they were *kind*? If he hoped to make Anna his duchess, though—which, thinking rationally about what he *wanted* in a wife, he still wasn't sure he did, but supposing he did—the world, Society, would want to know those things about her parents.

Did he want to make her his duchess? He just did not know. The desire that he felt for her was one thing. He could manage that. The love for her that he felt building inside him, though: he was not sure whether he could cope with that. Because what if something happened to her, as it had to his father and brothers in such quick succession? He couldn't bear to lose her. And what if he did indeed die young, like his brothers, as his mother feared he would, and Anna loved him the way he loved her, and she was left bereft? It did not bear thinking about; he was almost shuddering at the horror of it.

'Tell me about your father and brothers?' Anna asked at that exact moment.

Was she a mind reader, or was that a natural question following his to her?

'My father was unfashionably and unashamedly most

attached to his family and very much enjoyed spending time with us. He enjoyed hunting and shooting and fencing, and took my brothers and me out with him as soon as we were out of leading strings. And my brothers were both, I suppose, very similar to me in personality and tastes.'

He had also, he realised, described *them* as opposed to their status in life, but Anna *knew* who they were. And he had mentioned his father's activities, whereas after what Anna had said he was none the wiser about her parents' tastes.

'They sound wonderful,' she said. 'I'm so sorry for your loss.'

'And I for yours.' He reached out to squeeze her hand and she squeezed his back.

He was probably reading too much into her choice of words. It was after all difficult talking about relatives one mourned. Perhaps she had said all she could bear to say at this point.

When they reached Bruton Street, he felt a strong urge to ask Anna now when they could meet again. It was beginning to feel to him as though the days on which he did not see her were empty.

He did not ask, however.

'Thank you again; I very much enjoyed the afternoon,' he told her. And then he watched her inside before driving off.

He needed to restrain himself until he had made sure of his own intentions. He did not want to hurt her and so if he did not have serious intentions he should probably stop seeing her. She would be utterly ruined if anyone saw what they had done.

And, good God, he had run quite mad. After what they had done, he owed it to her—irrespective of his thoughts on love within marriage—to marry her. Of course he did. He should propose to her very soon. He…

Now was not the time, though.

He needed a little more time to think.

He should perhaps pay a call to Lady Derwent.

The next afternoon he was seated in Lady Derwent's drawing room wishing that he had called at almost *any* other time, or agreed in advance a particular time to see her; she had been taking tea with three dowagers when he arrived and they were all *extremely* interested to see him.

'Amscott, how are your dear mothers and sisters?' Lady Forcet asked him.

Time dragged as the ladies drew from him very small details about his family's health and whereabouts and marital intentions.

'None,' he said shortly in reference to his five youngest sisters.

Eventually, after he had wasted a good half hour of his life in her drawing room, Lady Derwent took pity on him and said, 'Perhaps we might drive in the park together, Amscott. You may call for me at half past four tomorrow.'

Twenty-five hours later, James was finally able to speak to Lady Derwent alone.

'I had expected you to bring your curricle,' she said as he handed her up into the chaise he had brought, assuming that she would not want to ride in a curricle. 'I am not in my dotage yet, thank you.'

He laughed. 'I must apologise. I will bear that in mind for any future drives we take together.'

As they moved forward, he opened his mouth to ask her immediately about Anna, but was thwarted when she began to talk to him about the weather. She continued onto the latest gossip from Court, and then the weather again, and then some exclamations about how bare the trees seemed now. And then the weather again.

Finally, she began to describe—in stunning detail—the exhibition at the Royal Academy that she had been to earlier in the week. She began with descriptions of what every lady she had seen there had been wearing, while James began to wonder if he would be able to speak at *all* during the drive, or whether this would be a wasted afternoon from the perspective of finding out a little more about Anna.

And then Lady Derwent moved on to talking about some of the paintings, before saying, 'My goddaughter would certainly appreciate the exhibition. Perhaps you should take her.'

Finally!

'Perhaps I should,' James said. 'I do not, however, know whether Miss Blake is particularly interested in art.'

'I am sure she would enjoy it.'

'Has Miss Blake visited many art exhibitions before now?'

'One or two only, I imagine.' Lady Derwent smiled at him. 'I commend you for hiding your frustration so admirably during the first part of our drive.'

'I assure you that I have enjoyed your company during the entirety of this afternoon,' James said cautiously.

'Fiddlesticks. The only reason that you wanted to see me was to ask me about Miss Blake, was it not?'

'A little,' said James, trying not to wince, 'but I am also enjoying the drive and hearing your views on other topics.'

'Gammon.' Lady Derwent rolled her eyes so thoroughly that James was worried she might give herself a headache. 'Enquire of me whatever you like about my goddaughter, and I will answer you where I am able and deem it acceptable.'

Good God. James was suddenly almost nervous. He had been trying to ask such questions for some time, and now he had carte blanche to ask what he liked. What if he did not like the answers? Also, was this really acceptable? To ask questions about Miss Blake to which she might not like him to know the answers?

It was not acceptable, he realised. He would *like* to find out everything about her, but he could not in all conscience go behind her back like this. He could not ask Lady Derwent a question about Anna that he would not ask her directly.

He was quite sure, however, that Lady Derwent had only Anna's best interests at heart.

Perhaps his best course of action was honesty.

In moderation. He was not going to disclose what had happened between him and Anna on their ice-tasting afternoons.

'In truth,' he said, hoping that he was indeed about to speak the truth, because he wouldn't like to lie to Lady Derwent, 'I did intend to ask you some questions about Miss Blake, but on reflection I find that I should not ask you anything about her that I would not ask her to her face. And therefore I do not have anything to ask about her.'

'I see.' Lady Derwent observed him for an unnervingly long time through her lorgnette, for so long in fact that James found himself struggling to keep his focus on his horses and the road.

Eventually, she cleared her throat and said, 'May I ask your intentions towards my goddaughter?'

James gave an involuntary twitch and caused one of his horses to stop for a moment, and the carriage to lurch a little.

'I must apologise,' he said, when he had them back under control a few moments later. 'I cannot remember the last time I drove so badly.'

'Perhaps you also cannot remember the last time someone asked you if you intended to marry their goddaughter or not.'

This time James laughed rather than jobbing his horses' mouths, which was an improvement.

'That is true,' he said.

'And what is your answer?'

'I…' This was not good. He should really have thought of this when he decided to call on Lady Derwent.

'Yes?'

'I admire Miss Blake very much,' he said. 'She is a most…admirable young woman.'

'Do you intend to propose to her, though? Do you love her?'

'I…' Good God. What if Lady Derwent relayed the import of this conversation to Anna? And what would Anna's thoughts be at this moment in time? 'I am not certain and—without wishing to sound arrogant and assuming that anyone to whom I might propose marriage would accept—I would not wish to raise anyone's hopes of a proposal—which of course they might or might not choose to accept or be happy about—before I knew myself what I intended.'

He did intend to propose, he was certain of that now, but he did not wish his proposal to be via Lady Derwent as proxy.

'So you called on me with the intention of asking about Anna? And then thought better of it because you did not feel it fair to ask about something that you would not ask her directly.'

James nodded ruefully. 'That is correct,' he said. 'I cannot ask you anything that Miss Blake would not choose to tell me herself.'

'That is laudable. If a little dull.'

'Thank you?'

Lady Derwent ignored him and continued, 'I am going to give you one important piece of information. I am also going to give you a warning.'

'Indeed?'

'I will begin with the warning. Do not trifle with my goddaughter's heart. She is a wonderful young lady and I should not like to see her upset.'

'I would not like to upset her,' James said.

'That is good. I understand that you have been seen with other young ladies, including Lady Catherine Rainsford. For everyone's sake, you would be wise to make your choice sooner rather than later.'

'Yes.'

Lady Derwent was, he had to admit, correct; and it

was right and proper that she should attempt to protect her goddaughter.

'I would not like to upset Miss Blake,' he repeated.

Lady Derwent ignored him again. 'The information that I think you might like to have concerns Anna's birth.'

James did of course wish to learn such information, but, the more he thought about it, the more uneasy he felt about betraying Anna's trust—such as she might have—and speaking about her in her absence.

'I'm not sure…' he began.

'Nonsense.' Lady Derwent spoke over him before he could finish his objection. 'She is the granddaughter of an earl.'

And there he had it, or part of it. Her background.

He couldn't tell whether he had been expecting that or not. Part of him, he realised, had worried that she might be of low birth, which would make marriage between them more difficult. His mother was a stickler for tradition and good breeding, although he hoped that her wish for him to be happy would transcend any feeling that the woman he married might not be of exactly the family his mother would have chosen. He had also, however, been quite sure all along that Anna was a lady.

'A particularly august earl,' Lady Derwent continued. 'Of a very old family. Anna's grandfather was the late Earl of Broome. The ninth earl.'

James frowned. He knew, distantly, of the Earl of Broome. The new—tenth—earl was young, younger than him. Perhaps something had happened within the family of the sort that he and his mother worried might happen if he, James, died without issue. Perhaps the earldom had passed to a distant cousin who had not provided for Anna on the death of her mother. The cur. If the man were in front of him now, James would want to throttle him. How could he live with the knowledge that his cousin was now forced to work as a governess? Surely the man could make her an allowance of enough to live modestly without working?

Perhaps he would ask his mother about the earl. Perhaps not, on second thought, or not until he had made up his mind exactly when—and how—he would propose to Anna.

Because, yes, of *course* he was going to propose to her. He had to. He had compromised a young lady of quality and it was irrelevant whether or not anyone else knew. *He* knew. He had to do the right thing by her.

Good God. He was going to propose to Anna. As soon as he could.

And if she accepted, they would marry. They would be husband and wife.

And that would be…well, it would be a lot of things.

It would be terrifying, because, obviously, due to the fact that she was wonderful in every way, he would end up—if he wasn't already—deeply in love with her. His wife. And so, if anything happened to her, he would be heartbroken, bereft.

But it would also be exhilarating, life-affirming, perfect… Because being married to Anna would enable him to see her every day: talk to her, laugh with her, make love to her, just *be* with her.

He would be the luckiest man alive.

He realised suddenly that he had been staring ahead while he thought, completely ignoring Lady Derwent.

'I must apologise,' he said. 'My thoughts were elsewhere. Thank you for letting me know.'

'There is no need to apologise. I presume you were thinking of my goddaughter.'

James inclined his head.

'I must remind you.' Her tone had hardened significantly. 'I would expect to hear either a happy announcement in relation to you and Anna, or nothing at all. That is to say: you must not trifle with her affections. If you do not intend to marry her, I would expect you no longer to spend any time with her. Her work as a governess does not preclude her from marrying and I do not wish her reputation to be sullied by you.'

'Of course.' James had nothing further to add, because he was certainly not going to tell Lady Derwent before he asked Anna that he hoped very much that Anna would like to marry him.

He would have liked Anna to have told him herself about her background, but he understood that it must be very hurtful and humiliating effectively being rejected by one's own family, and perhaps it was something that she did not feel she could discuss with anyone. Hopefully, in time, she would feel that she was able to confide in him—hopefully her husband.

Now he just needed to plan his proposal.

The next morning, after much thought, he sent a note inviting Anna to the opera that evening. She had mentioned in passing that she had never been, and he had been sure that, while she was not a woman to evince any self-pity, he had caught a wistful note in her voice.

He had been careful in his planning not to organise an

evening that might compromise her; he had also invited Lady Derwent—and had received her acceptance before he penned his invitation to Anna—as well as his mother, his married sister and her husband, and two or three other friends, and had told Anna that he was doing so.

He had thought long and hard about the timing of the opera trip. Should it be before or after he proposed—assuming she accepted the proposal? He had decided that it would be more comfortable for Anna to enter into a betrothal with him if she already knew his mother and sister a little better. And from their side, if they got to know her, they could not fail to like her, and he would wish his family and his wife to get on well together.

He was sure that Lady Derwent would then happily allow him to escort Anna home himself while she travelled in her own carriage.

He waited on tenterhooks for Anna's reply and was heartily relieved when he received an acceptance of his invitation within three hours of issuing it. Now he just needed to wait for the evening to come.

Chapter Eleven

Anna

Anna had just arrived back from her morning walk with the girls when she received James's card. As she had looked at the envelope and recognised his handwriting, her heart had—annoyingly—quickened, and she had decided to put it to one side and open it later. She had resolved yesterday evening not to continue her outings with him, however much she might like ice creams. And his company. And what they'd done together in the carriage each time.

She had been very lucky that no one had seen them on the three occasions that they had kissed—and more— and she couldn't risk being caught in such a compromising situation.

In addition, she had, she realised, developed feelings for James that were much stronger than mere liking, and she did not wish to have her heart broken. He would clearly not contemplate marrying her, as evidenced by his dallying with her in this way; she was sure that dukes did not do such things with young ladies of quality. Clearly, therefore, he knew her to be inferior to him socially, and that was why he had behaved the way he had. Equally clear was that he would need to marry and produce at least one heir relatively soon.

She did not wish to be heartbroken when he married someone else—Lady Catherine Rainsford for example—and she did not wish there to be any possibility that he might attempt to set her up as his mistress. Everyone knew that even the nicest of men behaved quite awfully in this regard.

So she hoped very much that he would be happy with whomever he married and she was glad—honestly, she was—that it wouldn't be her. Being deeply in love with one's own husband was a recipe for deep unhappiness. Dukes frequently had affairs outside marriage. Everyone knew that. Even if they did not abandon their wives in the way that her father had left her mother.

It was for the best, then, no longer to see each other. She did not wish to be any more heartbroken than she had to be.

Before she had opened the note, she had spoken quite sternly to herself. She would not accept whatever invitation it might contain.

Except…oh!

He had invited her to the opera with her godmother—who had apparently already indicated to him that she would be attending—together with his own mother and sister, and several other people.

Perhaps he held her in higher esteem than she had thought. It could not be possible—surely—that he would introduce her to his mother and sister in such a small group if he had dishonourable intentions towards her. Even though she was a governess and he had driven in the park with Lady Catherine between his two outings with Anna?

Or did he just regard her as a friend whom he would like to introduce to other friends? *Could* a duke openly have a governess as a friend?

Did he perhaps have intimate relations with all sorts of women? Anna had pushed that thought out of her mind as fast as it had entered; it did not make her feel good.

Whatever James's intentions, it must be quite unexceptionable to visit the opera with her own godmother as guests of a duke and his wider family and friends, and she would very much like to have the opportunity to go. There could be no risk on such an occasion of them succumbing to any temptation to kiss, so it could surely do no harm.

Once she had decided that, she had asked Lady Puntney if she would be happy for her to go. Her employer had, as usual, been quite delighted at her governess's moving in such august circles, and had told her 'dearest Miss Blake' that she must of course attend, and must enjoy herself as much as she could during her evenings off, so there had been nothing preventing Anna from accepting the invitation.

'Good evening, my dear,' Lady Derwent greeted her when—as agreed by an exchange of notes during the afternoon—Anna entered her godmother's carriage later that day. 'That mantle is most becoming; I am so glad that we bought it.'

The mantle in question was powder blue and lined and trimmed with fur and sewn with gold thread, and worn over a pale green silk evening dress. Both garments had been among Lady Derwent's more extravagant gifts to Anna, and she adored them both.

'Thank you. I am very grateful to you; I like it exceedingly.' She returned her godmother's embrace and said, 'You are also looking particularly fine this evening.'

Lady Derwent adjusted her own mantle into place and then spread her heavily beringed hands in front of her and regarded them with a complacent air.

'Yes, I think I am,' she said, which made them both laugh.

Laughing with her reminded Anna of laughing with James.

And this was silly. Really, *anything* nice reminded her of him. She wondered… She didn't want to wonder. She should *not* wonder; even if he did for some strange reason perhaps wish to…well, she couldn't even think it, but if he did wish something honourable, she was sure he would change his mind if he knew about the scandal of her parents' elopement and the fact that her father had been a groom.

If it began to look as though his intentions really might be honourable, she would have to tell him about her parents, as soon as possible.

The fact that he was introducing her to his mother did indicate that…

No, she mustn't think it.

She must, however, decide whether, should such a

thing occur, she would disclose the truth about her parents or just say no with no explanation.

When they arrived at the Theatre Royal, where they were to watch the opera, James was waiting in the road to meet them.

As he handed Anna down from the carriage, he applied just a little more pressure to her hand than might be usual, and fixed her with a particular look which made her feel quite warm inside; the look seemed to signal that he was extremely pleased to see her. A small smile was playing about his lips as he looked at her, and his eyes were focused on hers, as though she was the only other person that existed in his world.

The way he was looking at her was actually making her feel quite breathless.

'I am particularly pleased to see you here this evening,' he told her.

Anna had no words other than, 'Thank you,' accompanied by a shiver of pleasure.

As they made their way to his box, the hordes in the opera house's foyer parted easily for them due to James's broad shoulders and natural air of command. Anna could not remember a time when she had felt more protected within a crowd. It was a sensation that anyone would surely revel in.

The box was entirely velvet and gilt and felt beautifully luxurious. Glancing up, Anna saw that the ceiling was also very intricately decorated, with blue panels, relieved by white and enriched by gold.

James's entire *life* was luxury. She wondered briefly how he would feel about her if he knew that after her

mother's death before Lady Derwent had effectively rescued her she had been living in a very small and somewhat damp cottage with a friend of her mother's, a Miss
Shepson, another gentlewoman who had fallen on hard
times, and had been forced to take in sewing to try to
earn a few pennies so that she had money enough to eat.
Heating had been a luxury she could not often afford,
so both ladies had enjoyed the summer months considerably more than the winter ones.

'Miss Blake, you have already met my mother, the
dowager duchess. I am not sure you are acquainted with
my sister Lady Mallow and her husband, Lord Mallow.'

'I am very pleased to meet you.' Lady Mallow patted
the empty chair next to her. 'Come and sit next to me so
that we may talk more easily. You must call me Sybilla.'

'Thank you. And you must call me Anna.'

She and Sybilla exchanged mutual smiles, and immediately began a very comfortable cose; it quickly felt as
though they had known each other for quite some time.

Just before the opera—Mozart's *The Magic Flute*—
began, James made his way to the seat next to Anna's,
on the other side from Sybilla, and Anna could not help
feeling that there could be no more enjoyable way to
be seated. Other than alone with James in his carriage
but that was quite inappropriate and should not—could
not—happen again, and she should not even think about
it.

'Are you too warm?' James asked her in an under-
tone. 'Your cheeks are a little red.'

'Oh, no! I just…' She wondered what he would say—
or indeed *do*—if she told him that she had been blush-
ing at her own scandalous thoughts, involving him… 'I

am very well, thank you, and it is the perfect temper-
ature in here. I am very much looking forward to the
performance.'

'I am pleased to hear it. And I too am looking forward to it; I shall very much enjoy watching it with you.'

Sitting next to James in the near darkness, knowing
that he was so close to her, almost able to touch him
without moving far, knowing what he felt like and how
it felt when he touched her but prevented from doing
anything of that nature by the presence of his sister on
her other side and the others in their group around them
was quite overwhelming.

The performance was wonderful. Anna was trans-
ported to ancient Egypt and fully engrossed in the story.
Knowing that she was sharing it with James made it an
even more intense experience.

When the interval came, she realised that she was almost tearful from the beauty of the story and the singing. It was blissful to be able to discuss and exclaim
over the performance with James and his sister, and to
witness their funning with each other and the sibling
bond they shared.

A few minutes into the interval, there was some
movement around the box. Sybilla rose to go and speak
to a cousin, and another lady seated herself in her place.

James had just started saying something, but was
interrupted by the lady in Sybilla's seat leaning very
rudely across Anna as though she were a piece of furni-
ture rather than an actual person, and saying, 'I should
love to hear your views on this particular production of
The Magic Flute, Your Grace.'

Anna couldn't work out whether she was more annoyed by the rudeness or sad about the very strong reminder that James—the lofty Duke of Amscott—could not possibly contemplate, even if he wanted to, marrying a woman like Anna. If someone were this rude when they believed her to be of acceptable birth, then how much ruder or dismissive would they be if they knew about her parents?

She glanced up at James and saw that his eyes were suddenly like flints and his expression rigid.

'I believe that introductions have not been performed,' he said in chilly tones. 'Miss Blake, this is Mrs Chilcott, an acquaintance of my mother's. Mrs Chilcott, this is Miss Blake, a particular friend of my family's and goddaughter of Lady Derwent.'

Anna smiled at him and tried not to feel horrified about the fact that her presence had caused James to be in this position.

'Oh. Miss Blake. Yes. Forgive me… I'm not quite sure…' The lady raised one eyebrow in a very haughty fashion. Anna stared back at her, quite taken aback at her rudeness.

'Not sure about…?' James's voice was now so cold it could have frozen water. 'As I said, Miss Blake is Lady Derwent's goddaughter and is also known by my mother. I am surprised that you do not know her, but she is recently arrived in town, and perhaps you were not at my mother's ball, where you would have met her.'

'Of course I was at your mother's ball,' the lady trilled. 'You and I conversed for quite ten minutes.'

'Forgive me.' The Duke's voice was still as hard as

stone. 'It was a busy evening for me and I spoke to a great many people.'

Anna did her best to smile as the lady began to brush over her rudeness in the face of the Duke's evident distaste for it, but it was difficult. Quite aside from the fact that men were not to be trusted, *this* was why she would never be able to marry someone of his standing in Society. When it became known that she was the product of her mother's scandalous elopement with one of Anna's grandfather's grooms, she would regularly be the subject of this kind of rudeness, and it would be very difficult for her husband. How long would it be until he tired of the difficulty?

'Indeed,' said James for about the fifth time in response to yet another opening sally from Mrs Chilcott.

Eventually, Mrs Chilcott rose and said, 'It has been most pleasant to converse.'

Anna smiled blandly and James inclined his head the merest fraction, and Mrs Chilcott turned and left in what could only be described as a flouncing manner.

'I'm so sorry,' James said. 'I abhor such rudeness.'

'No, no; it was my presence that caused it.'

'Well, it *was* your presence, but it was not *you*. Many people envy a young lady who is singled out by an unmarried duke of marriageable age.'

Anna screwed her face up a little. 'I am not sure it is that; I think it is rather that she did not deem me a suitable person with whom to converse.'

'Nonsense. That could never be the case.' James's smile was so warm that Anna felt her eyes to be suddenly moist. 'Let us not waste any more time talking about someone neither of us knows; instead let me introduce you further to my mother.'

He drew Anna over to the duchess, who was conversing with Lady Derwent, and soon had all three of the ladies laughing with his observations on the evening, before asking Anna, 'What aspect of the opera have you enjoyed the most so far?'

'That is a very hard question to answer,' she said. 'It's all wonderful. The theatre itself, the way the set on the stage is designed, the costumes, the music, and of course the singing and acting. I would find it very difficult to choose a favourite. The whole combine to make it a truly intoxicating experience.'

The duchess nodded. 'I agree. Too many people come to the opera merely to see and be seen. We must not forget that we are very lucky to witness such wonderful art on the stage.'

'That is very true, Leonora,' said Lady Derwent, and the two matrons smiled at each other. From what Anna had heard, this was a remarkable achievement on the part of James.

The three ladies found themselves in strong agreement on a variety of topics, and Anna enjoyed their conversation so much that she was almost sorry when the second half of the opera began.

As they re-seated themselves in preparation to begin watching again, James said sotto voce to Anna, 'I'm so pleased that you and my mother have established such a rapport, and that you seem to have struck up an immediate friendship with Sybilla.'

A shiver ran all the way down Anna from the back of her neck almost to her toes. It was nice—she thought—

to know that it was unlikely he would do her the dishonour of wishing to set her up as his mistress; no one sane would introduce their paramour to their own mother. However, his clearly wishing that she and his mother become better acquainted did indicate that he might indeed be considering proposing to her.

If she were an entirely different woman, who could ever dare to entrust her heart and independence to a man, and if she were from an entirely different, scandal-free family, that might be—would be—wonderful.

But as it was it was quite awful. Rejecting him *would* be for the best because it would protect her from being tossed aside by him at some point in the future.

She would have to tell him about her parents. She *couldn't* just turn him down with no explanation. If she didn't have the opportunity to do so this evening, she would ask him for a short meeting as soon as possible.

She didn't want the opera to end. In itself, it was a wonderful spectacle, but the reason she wanted it to continue for ever was that she was quite sure that it would be the last time that she would have the opportunity to spend time with James like this. And that was deeply, deeply sad.

She didn't want to be sad. She should make the most of these last few moments, enjoy the way that when anything particularly dramatic happened he turned to her, enjoy the way their glances caught, enjoy being able to look at his handsomeness, enjoy the sensation that for now, this evening, he was *hers*.

And when he smiled at her—in that particular, just-for-her way that she *adored*—she should just drink it in, for one last time, rather than stupidly feeling her eyes fill with tears.

Eventually, too soon, the performance was over, and Anna didn't want to think about the imminent end to the evening, so instead she busied herself with chatter to the people around them.

And then everyone began to take their leave.

As she was about to thank James for a wonderful evening and say good-night—knowing that this was the last time she would see him before their friendship ended—he turned towards her godmother and spoke in a low voice to her.

Then he turned back to Anna and spoke quietly to her. 'Lady Derwent is happy for me to escort you home in my carriage; I have something most particular to ask you.'

Ohhhh, goodness.

Oh, dear.

Well. She couldn't say no to the suggestion without making a scene and drawing attention to them in a way that could do neither of them any good. And it would be the ideal opportunity for her to tell him about her parents.

So after a pause, she just said, 'Thank you.'

She would tell him everything as soon as they got into the carriage and thank him personally for the lovely times they had spent together, and then he would take her back to Bruton Street and that would be the end of things. She should not be devastated at the thought that she would not see him again; she should be grateful that she had experienced Gunter's and the opera and…all that *pleasure*…with him.

* * *

When they reached James's carriage, he held his hand out for her to take as she ascended the steps, and held on to hers for a little longer than necessary, looking into her eyes as he did so. He had his lips half pressed together, half smiling, as though he was full of happiness.

Which made Anna feel the exact opposite.

She purposely avoided his eye while she was seating herself on the forward-facing velvet-upholstered seat of the carriage, both because now that the end was so near, even just looking at him was painful, and because she didn't wish to lead him to think that she was hoping for or would accept a proposal.

She was tempted to sit right in the middle of the seat to imply that he should sit opposite her rather than next to her, and then moved towards the right-hand corner at the last minute, worried that he would still sit next to her and they would then be far too close to each other.

He closed the carriage door behind him and did indeed sit down on the same seat as her, angling his body towards hers.

She lifted her regard from the floor to him and nearly gasped at the expression on his face. It was so…well, adoring. He was just *looking*, as though his entire being was focused on her and only her, and it was so much she could barely breathe. If only she hadn't been born of scandal; if only she could trust that he wouldn't cast her aside, as her father had done to her mother. She had to tell him. And she would do so, as soon as they set off and she was certain that no one could hear their words.

And then, before the carriage had even shown any

signs of moving, James reached forward and took her hands in his, and said, 'Anna.'

'Oh,' said Anna. 'James.' No, that wasn't the right thing to say. He'd sounded as though he was speaking in a very romantic kind of way, and so did she. And she mustn't. 'James, I…'

'Anna, I have a very particular question to ask you and I'm not sure I can wait any longer.' He moved a little closer to her so that their knees were touching.

Even though she *knew* she was about to put an end to all of this, Anna's insides were turning to liquid just at his touch, which was just so silly.

She felt the carriage begin to move forward and wondered how long it would take to get back to Bruton Street. Not very long.

He leaned forward and kissed her lightly on the lips and she wanted *so much* to reach for him, pull him close to her, kiss him properly. But no. She must not and she needed to stop him before he said anything that he would clearly regret later.

She wriggled backwards a little, and said, 'James, no, I…' She had to tell him *now*.

'I'm sorry; you are of course right. We should not… yet.'

Before she could react further, he lowered himself to one knee, re-gathered her hands in his, turned them over and pressed his lips hard to each of her palms in turn, before saying, 'Anna, dearest Anna, will you marry me?'

Oh!

No.

No.

She was—for this one moment—the luckiest woman in the world.

But really, she felt like the *un*luckiest.

She had so much she needed to say, immediately, but all she could manage was, 'Oh, oh, *James.*'

He kissed her hands again, before turning them back over and drawing them close to his chest and saying, his voice hoarse all of a sudden, 'Is that… Might I hope that that is a yes?'

Oh, no. This was truly, truly awful.

Anna closed her eyes. For one long moment she wished that she could just accept. But at some point she would *have* to tell him about her parents. And men being what they were, he would no doubt pull out of the engagement at that point. Better for both of them for her to tell him now.

She took a deep, juddering breath before trying to pull her hands away.

'I'm so sorry.' Her words were little more than a whisper; it was as though her voice did not work properly any more. 'I cannot marry you.'

He froze for a moment, and then let go of her hands and bowed his head briefly before slowly rising and sitting down on the seat behind him, opposite Anna.

The space between them suddenly seemed huge.

'I'm so sorry,' he said in a horribly croaky voice, after an awful silence. 'I had perhaps misunderstood; I believed… That is to say… Of course. Might I… There is of course no obligation to reply but might I ask your reason?' His voice, his demeanour seemed horrifyingly diminished somehow.

Anna had never seen him like this before and it was

dreadful. Previously he'd always seemed so big and strong—he *was* big and strong—but big and strong in spirit as well as body. He'd always seemed in command of every situation, confident, powerful.

It was terrible to think that her words could have reduced him somehow, and she very much needed to explain to him that her reason did not relate to *him*, it related to *her*.

She couldn't believe that at any point she had imagined that she might refuse a proposal without giving him a reason. She could never in reality bear him to think that she might not love him. No one—pauper or duke—should be led to believe that they were unlovable.

'Of course I will tell you the reason,' she said, despising herself for the fact that her voice was wobbling.

She drew a deep breath.

'I am not someone you can marry,' she told him when she was certain that she had command of her voice. 'I am not an appropriate wife for a duke.' She felt a tear dribble down her cheek and wiped it away with her fingers. 'I want you to know that any woman—lady—would be very lucky to marry you. It is not that you are not an acceptable husband; it is entirely that I am not an acceptable wife.'

'Anna. No.' James rose from his bench and moved back to sit next to her. 'That is not true.' He put his arm round her and pulled her against him with one arm before with his other hand very gently wiping the tears that were now coursing freely down her face.

Anna gave a gigantic sniff and said, 'It is.'

'No.' He pulled her even closer and kissed her forehead. 'Never. You are funny, kind, interesting, clever, wonderful, and of course very beautiful. You have all the attributes that any man could ever desire in a wife.'

Anna sniffed even harder, but nothing could prevent her tears now. She couldn't imagine a more wonderful set of compliments. All given under false pretences, of course, because she was not who he thought she was.

James wiped her tears again with his fingers, and then, taking her chin in his hand, gently turned her face towards his and then lowered his mouth to hers.

Anna allowed herself to return his kiss for one long—blissful—moment, before drawing back a little and saying, 'No, you don't understand, I can't.'

'I'm sorry. Of course.' James kept his arm round her but didn't attempt to kiss her again.

'I need to tell you something.' She took another breath, wiped under her eyes again, and squared her shoulders within the circle of his arm. 'You are wonderful. I have enjoyed spending time with you so very much.'

'Thank you. And I you.'

'I do very much wish you to know that.' She had to tell him *now* but it was hard to get the words out.

'I have also enjoyed myself with you very greatly.' He smiled at her and it felt as though her heart might crack.

When he reached for her again, she allowed herself for one moment to be drawn into his arms, to feel one last time the strength of his arms around her, his body against hers. If only she could stay here for ever.

As she clung to him, her face buried against his chest, she heard him say, his voice sounding impossibly deep, 'Anna, I love you, so very, very much.'

'I love you too,' she whispered, and then she lifted

her face to his, even though she shouldn't, because she couldn't prevent herself.

It was inevitable that they would kiss. There was passion, fire, and on Anna's side huge regret and sadness at what she knew was coming.

They kissed urgently and hard, before their hands found each other's bodies and they began to fumble with clothing, fast, telling each other to be quick because the journey was not that long.

Soon they were both hot and panting and, *oh*, the incredible pleasure of the cleverness of James's fingers and tongue. Anna was almost tempted to *beg* him to do *everything* with her this time—one final time—but sanity—a tiny modicum at least—prevailed.

As they helped each other return their clothing to a semblance of modesty, laughing and kissing as they did so, James said again, 'I love you so much.' The happiness and laughter in his voice was heart-rending, because he was about to be told something he clearly wasn't going to want to hear.

And that thought brought Anna to her senses.

'James, we shouldn't have, *I* shouldn't have… I'm so sorry. I have to tell you.' As she spoke, she felt the carriage come to a halt. 'But I think we've arrived. I need to tell you now.'

'My coachman will not open the door; we have as long as we need.' He was still smiling at her, clearly unaware that she was about to burst the bubble of happiness he seemed to be wearing, clearly assuming that her earlier refusal had perhaps been maidenly confusion.

'I am just going to say it,' she told him. 'I have been trying to preface it with softer explanations, and that led to what just happened, which really should not have happened again.'

James's eyes had narrowed and his smile had dropped as she spoke.

'Yes?' he asked.

Anna looked away from him for a moment, and then back into his eyes.

'My father was my grandfather's second groom. My mother and he fell in love and they ran away together. It caused a great scandal, and my grandfather disowned my mother and they never saw each other again. We lived quietly in the country, in some penury.'

James shook his head, his brow furrowing, as though he couldn't immediately understand her words. 'I... I'm afraid...'

'I should have mentioned: it's even worse than that, if that were possible. I was born six months after my parents ran away together. The scandal was great. My grandfather disowned my mother. Some of her friends remained loyal to her, in particular my wonderful god-mother, Lady Derwent, but most did not. Things became even worse when I was about nine, when my father left us. He now lives in Canada. I wrote to him when my mother died, but he showed no interest. When I referred to our having lost him, I meant that he had abandoned us.' Anna looked hard at James. The duke. His face had become like a mask, with no emotion showing. 'As you can see,' she pursued, 'I am not someone the Duke of Amscott can marry.'

James was entirely silent. He had released her from his arms and was sitting, with his hands on his knees, just staring at the floor of the carriage.

Anna felt very, very cold, and quite mortified at the way her dress was still in some disarray. How could she have touched him, allowed him to touch her in that way only a few minutes ago? Now it just felt sordid, embarrassing.

This was exactly like she imagined her mother's experience had been, when she'd been rejected by her own father when she got pregnant, and then rejected by her own husband when times were hard.

She realised now that a tiny part of her had hoped that the duke might say that he did not care about her birth. But of course he cared, and was rejecting her. That was what men did.

When, after what felt a very long time, the duke raised his head, she saw that his eyes had gone unpleasantly hard.

'You lied to me,' he stated.

Anna felt herself stiffen. It mattered to her, she realised, what James thought of her probity. And it mattered, more broadly, how men treated women, and how more privileged people treated less privileged ones.

She was not going to be accused of something she had not done. Yes, her birth was undesirable, but no, she had not lied. 'No, I did not. Obviously I did go to your ball in the guise of Lady Maria, but when I did that I was not lying to *you*; it was, as you know, just a silly deception. And since then I have not lied to you at all. I have not at any point pretended to be anything other than an impecunious governess who has had the great good fortune to be sponsored by Lady Derwent but who otherwise cannot take any place in Society.'

James's lips had formed into a hard line. 'You must have known what I intended. And yet you said nothing.'

'I believe that that is unfair,' Anna said. 'I saw you driving in the park with Lady Catherine Rainsford earlier in the week. Why would I presume that you were intending to marry me?'

'I was driving with her because my mother arranged it. It was not my choice. And you and I had already been intimate by then.'

'I could not have known that it was your mother who had arranged your outing. And—' her voice was suddenly shaking with anger now, at the injustice of *his* anger '—if I should have assumed that our being *intimate* would cause you to propose to me, should not that proposal have come immediately?'

'You should have told me sooner,' he repeated.

She glared at him. It was suddenly like looking at a stranger.

A stranger with whom she had had really the best times of her life and who had just proposed marriage to her.

No, he had not in fact proposed marriage to *her*; he had proposed marriage to someone else, a woman he had thought suitable to be his bride. A woman of excellent birth who had sadly fallen on hard times but who had no scandal in her background.

There could be no point in continuing this dreadful conversation.

And, frankly, if he could be this unreasonable, she didn't even care any longer what he thought of her. Because this proved that her fears had been right, that men's affections were always conditional and easily lost.

'Goodbye,' she said. 'Thank you for—' she could not call it a nice evening; it had begun gloriously but ended terribly '—thank you.' It had, after all, been kind of him to invite her to the opera.

'Allow me to help you down,' James said stiffly. 'Excuse me.'

His arm brushed Anna's for a moment as he reached for the door handle, and she had to swallow a sob at how it was now extremely awkward for them to touch at all.

Once out of the carriage, he held his arm out for Anna to support her as she descended the steps. She placed two fingers very gingerly on his arm and released it as soon as she was sure that she wouldn't trip; touching him in any way felt very wrong now.

'Thank you again,' she said in her most formal tone.

'It was a pleasure,' he said, with great insincerity. 'Good night.'

Anna nodded and then began to walk up the steps towards the house, before suddenly freezing.

James—she must begin to think of him as *the duke* again, rather than in such familiar terms—had looked incredibly angry, and perhaps hurt, and seemed still to believe that she had purposely deceived him. What if he told someone else her secret and the Puntneys found out and she lost her job?

She turned back in his direction. 'Your Grace.'

He turned round instantly. 'Miss Blake?'

She very much did not wish to have to do this. But she *needed* her employment and must swallow her pride.

'I am a devoted governess and irrespective of my birth I do have the education and knowledge to instruct my charges,' she said. 'If I lose this position I will be destitute. I would be very grateful if you would undertake not to discuss this—or anything we *did*—with anyone.'

'Of course.' He was extremely tight-lipped. 'I should not dream of it.'

'Thank you.' She must get inside and up to her bed-chamber before she allowed herself to *sob* as she felt she was about to do. 'Good night, then.'

'Good night.'

And that was that.

Chapter Twelve

James

James had cried at the deaths of his father and his two brothers but other than that he couldn't remember the last time he had even had a tear in his eye.

Now, watching Anna—Miss Blake—walk up the steps, her slim back held very straight, he didn't just have a lump in his throat; he felt as though he could easily spend a considerable amount of time bawling his eyes out.

He had expected this evening to be one of the happiest of his life. Instead, this. A real grief.

Suddenly, he took two steps forward. He couldn't let her go inside without apologising. He had accused her of lying. She was right: she had not lied to him. He had *felt* in that moment that she had, but she hadn't. He had lashed out from the depths of his misery, and that was a terrible thing to have done.

'Anna.' His voice sounded low, urgent to his own ears.

She froze for a moment, and then turned round, very slowly.

'Yes?'

'I am so sorry,' he said, in a rush to get his words out, feeling as though she might turn and slip inside at any moment. 'I apologise for having accused you of lying to me. I know that you did not. I am aware that much of our…relationship…has been instigated by me, and that you would not have been aware of my intentions initially. And you did of course tell me the truth as soon as I made my intentions clear. I must apologise from my side for not having made them clear immediately, the first time we…did things that we should not have done. I am sorry for everything and I would like you to know that I have very much enjoyed all our time together.' He was babbling, he realised, trying to make the situation better.

'I love you,' he concluded.

'I love you too,' she said. 'I wish you very well. Goodbye.'

And then, while he stood there staring, aghast but his mind strangely frozen so that he could not work out what he should do or say next, she turned back round and continued her way up the steps.

When she closed the front door behind her, it felt as though a door was closing on an unlived chapter of the rest of his life that he hadn't known he wanted until he met her.

He stared at the door for a long time, before turning and telling his coachman in a flat voice that he would walk.

And then he set off down the road. Walking felt like an extraordinary effort, as though his limbs had become entirely leaden.

God. Only perhaps twenty minutes ago, he and Anna had kissed, touched each other intimately, the precursor, he had assumed, to what would be blissful full lovemaking when they were married. And now...now they were entirely separate, and there could be no reason for them to see each other again.

His mind felt as leaden as his limbs.

He couldn't go home yet. He turned left instead of right and began an aimless walk through the streets of Mayfair as he tried to make sense of how he felt.

He hadn't wanted to marry at all but he needed to do so in order to produce an heir to secure his mother and sisters' futures.

If he had to get married, he had been adamant that he hadn't wished to fall in love with his wife, because he hadn't wanted to put himself in a position where he might experience further loss.

The entire reason that he'd planned to marry now was to take care of his mother and sisters. His wife being known to be someone of such scandalous background could cause his own family to be embroiled in the scandal. What if that harmed his sisters' marriage prospects? What if *they* then ended up as governesses, or in undesirable marriages? What if one of them, for example, fell in love with an impecunious curate as Lady Maria had done? In that instance, if she was no longer under the protection of a powerful man, could it cause her problems if her sister-in-law were someone from a scandalous background? What if he married Anna and they had a son and then he, James, died young as his brothers had, when their son was still a minor? Would Society accept Anna as effectively a regent for a child duke?

Life was damned difficult for women and it was a huge responsibility having so many sisters to set on a happy path in life, not to mention his mother, who had borne so much grief with so much dignity.

He could not bear any of his sisters to have to become a governess.

He did not like the thought of Anna being a governess.

He also didn't like the thought of her being sad. She'd cried so much. She'd looked stricken.

He'd been awful to her. He'd accused her of lying. She hadn't lied. She hadn't even knowingly misled him. She couldn't have suspected until recently that he planned to ask her to marry him. If doing things together that would clearly compromise her had caused him to propose, why had he not done so immediately? How could she have known that he would suddenly realise that he should, and that in that moment he was happy to do so because he loved her?

At least he had apologised to her. But the fact remained that he had done things with her that one should not do with a lady of quality who was not one's wife. She *was* a lady of quality; her grandfather was an earl. She hadn't told him that. She had only told him that her father was a groom. She had not tried to protect herself in any way.

He'd been right about never wanting to fall in love: this hurt damnably.

So maybe this was for the best. As long as Anna wasn't too miserable.

Chapter Thirteen

Anna

Anna awoke the next morning lying on top of her bed still in her opera-visiting finery, her head feeling as though a metal clamp was squeezing it and her mouth as though she'd munched through the feathers in her eiderdown during her sleep.

As she blinked painfully dry eyes, she remembered that she'd walked blindly through the house and dissolved into tears the second she'd closed her bedchamber door behind her. Eventually, after much revisiting of painful conversations and misery in her head, she had gone to sleep there without changing out of her gown.

She had been very naïve, she realised. During the early hours of the night she had admitted to herself that she *had* actually hoped that James would propose to her *and* that he would somehow convince her that the scandal surrounding her parents did not matter. But of course it mattered, and of course James—the duke—could not ignore it. Her grandfather had abandoned her mother. Her father had not been the best of husbands to her mother. She knew that men expected women to adhere to higher standards than those to which they themselves adhered, and if they fell short—often through no fault of their own—they did not support them.

Really, she was lucky that things had come to a head now and that the farce of their friendship had ended.

It did hurt very much, though. As did her head.

She *really* did not want to look after young children this morning. She didn't really want to do anything. But if she *had* to do something, it would be much more akin to crawling behind a large rock and hiding there than plastering a smile on her face and attempting to instil discipline and knowledge into someone else's children, however generous a salary she was being paid to do it.

She was ready for breakfast—which Lady Puntney had kindly decreed from the beginning she should take with the family—only a little later than usual. Her looking glass had told her that her face was unusually pale and that the smile that she practised was sadly lacking in authenticity, but she hoped that no one would notice.

She managed to force down some toast and some tea, and discovered that the old adage that food and drink always made you feel better was absolute nonsense. She just felt now as though she was going to be sick. She wasn't sure whether her nausea was due to tiredness or misery or both, but it wasn't helping.

Two hours of instruction on arithmetic followed by some handwriting practice just increased the headache that accompanied her nausea, but it was very helpful to be occupied so that she did not have to be alone with her thoughts.

She and the children took their usual Hyde Park walk later in the morning, and as they reached the pond they liked to walk around, Anna realised that the fresh air was doing her some good; it was clearing her head a little, and looking at the trees and birds was an excellent reminder that life was bigger than just one man. She *would* be happy again, and she *would* make a good life for herself. She was lucky to have this employment, after all, and she was lucky to have Ladies Derwent and Maria as good friends.

By the time they arrived back at Bruton Street, Anna was still feeling deeply miserable, but she had pulled herself together sufficiently to enjoy the company of the children and to be sure that she really could recover from this; it would be a temporary misery.

As she was removing her brown wool pelisse, the one she wore when she was performing her governess role, Morcambe, the butler, said, 'Lady Puntney would like to speak to you in the library.'

Anna had been looking down as she unfastened buttons, but glanced up at his face in surprise, because the tone of his voice was odd, quite cold. She almost gasped out loud at the look on his face. He had always behaved very paternally towards her, and had always had a smile for her and often a word of advice, but now he was entirely unsmiling, and staring at her almost insolently.

A cold dread began to creep over her as she stared back at him. What had happened?

'Thank you,' she said, mortified to hear her own voice shake a little. She gave herself a little shake and then said, in a much stronger voice, thank goodness, 'I shall go to her directly.'

'See that you do,' Morcambe said, and Anna nearly gasped again at the rudeness.

A minute later, purposely having taken her time, to persuade herself that she could not be intimidated by Morcambe—but in reality really quite terrified by the change in his demeanour—she entered the library.

'Please close the door.' Lady Puntney was standing behind a writing table. When Anna had closed the door, she indicated a chair in front of the table, and said, 'Please sit down.'

Anna seated herself, feeling quite wild with fear now, as though her head might explode from inside.

Lady Puntney sat down too, and clasped her hands in front of her.

'I am sorry about this,' she began. And then she paused, for a very long time, while Anna swallowed hard.

Perhaps they no longer needed a governess. Although why then would Morcambe have been so insolent in his manner towards her? Surely he should have been more sympathetic?

'I have, as you know, been very pleased with your service.' Lady Puntney's voice faltered. 'The children have very much liked you and indeed I have too. However…' She paused again as Anna blinked to dispel sudden moistness in her eyes. Clearly, she was being asked to leave for some reason. She *needed* a job, though, and this one was better than any other she might hope to get.

'The problem is…' Lady Puntney cleared her throat. 'That is to say…' She unclasped her hands and pressed her fingertips together and then re-clasped them. 'I do not wish to be unfair.'

Then please keep me on, Anna screamed inside. Externally, she kept her face immobile and concentrated on not crying.

'Mrs Clarke told me this morning that she had overheard something last night of which she felt it her duty to inform me.'

Anna went very cold all over.

Lady Puntney pressed her lips together before continuing, 'She told me that you had had a conversation on the doorstep late last night with the Duke of Amscott that clearly indicated that you have had some form of intimacy with him.'

Oh, no, no, no. Mrs Clarke was the Puntneys' housekeeper. What exactly had she heard? What had they said after they left the privacy of the carriage? Oh, no. This had happened because she had implored the duke not to tell anyone about what had happened between them. How *stupid* of her. Or perhaps it was his apology that Mrs Clarke had heard. Whichever, Anna had been stupidly, *stupidly* rash spending any time with him whatsoever.

She shook her head, speechless.

'Are you able to tell me that this was a mistake?' Lady Puntney continued.

'I...' Anna wanted so much to lie. Would it hurt a living soul if she *did* lie? She didn't think it would. She *was* a good governess; she cared about the children and she felt that she was educating them well. She was *not* a debauched person. She would not influence them badly in any way. She didn't like lying, especially to someone who had treated her as well as Lady Puntney had. But could it hurt anyone if she denied it? She wouldn't want to get Mrs Clarke into trouble for having invented something that she had not in fact invented. What should she say? 'I…'

'Miss Blake! Your hesitation tells me everything I need to know. I had hoped to be told that Mrs Clarke was mistaken. I am distraught.' Lady Puntney was indeed twisting her hands most agitatedly and her eyes looked moist, but it was hard to imagine that she could be as distraught as was Anna.

Anna took a deep, juddering breath. She could not allow herself to dissolve in tears or indeed to say nothing; she had to find some words to explain her situation reasonably, if Lady Puntney would allow her. And then, obviously, she would almost certainly still ask her to leave, but at least she would hopefully not then think ill of her for ever.

'I met the duke at his mother's ball at the beginning of the Season,' she said.

Lady Puntney nodded, as though she wanted to hear more, and Anna realised that of course she wasn't going to refuse to listen to her; she would be agog to hear any gossip about the duke. Well, Anna was not going to give her any gossip, including about her masquerade as Lady Maria, but she would do her best to clear her own name. Just in case. She was not going to volunteer the details about her parents, because that could do her no good and was nobody else's business, and if she was lucky Mrs Clarke would not have overheard that.

If Mrs Clarke *had* heard that, Anna would have to obtain a post far from London if she were to continue as a governess. Most families wished for governesses at least as well-born as they were—just a lot more impecunious.

She should continue her story.

'At the ball, we danced twice and spoke for a while. Subsequently he asked me to go to Gunter's, as you know, and to the opera. And yesterday evening after the opera he escorted me home and we had—' she was almost choking on the words '—a small disagreement and are no longer friends.'

'Mrs Clarke gained the impression that you and the duke had, in her recital of what passed between you, "done" some things together.'

'We, no, that is…'

'I must tell you that she then felt herself obliged to question the staff and a number of them were suspicious, and disclosed that there have been strong whisperings about you and the duke. They had assumed that if you were…exchanging intimacies with him…you were perhaps secretly betrothed.'

Anna closed her eyes for a moment.

'I am afraid,' Lady Puntney said, 'that, even though you might be innocent of anything untoward, there will now be questions about you in people's minds, and that could extend to me and to my daughters. And I have to be prudent.'

'So,' asked Anna slowly, 'even if you knew things that people had said were just rumours, you would still feel that you had to act on them as though they were truth?'

Lady Puntney stared at her for a long time and then nodded. 'Yes, I think perhaps I would have to. For my family's sake. Such is the world in which we live. My status is not sufficiently high to withstand any kind of scandal.'

Anna nodded. Of course Lady Puntney had to think of her daughters' future, and they could not have a governess to whom was attached any scandal.

And, of course, the scandal was *true*. And Lady Puntney didn't even know about Anna's parents, or the extent of the scandal that *might* attach to Anna now.

She paused and then continued, 'Miss Blake— Anna—I very much like you. I do not know what has happened between you and the duke. I must confess— speaking very frankly—that I had hoped on your behalf that perhaps the duke's interest in you might lead to marriage. I believe that it is very wrong that any indiscretion between you means that you must lose your employment while he loses nothing.' She sniffed. 'I do wish that I did not have to let you go. But I am afraid that I have to think of my family and our reputation. Servants do talk. And others might have heard.'

Anna bowed her head. 'I understand.'

'Anna, I will do what I can. I will not tell anyone about this, and I will provide you with a reference so that you may find another position. Perhaps, though, it would be best for you to move to another part of the country so that rumours do not follow you via my servants. I do not like to think that they gossip widely, but one must be realistic about human nature.'

'Thank you,' Anna managed to say before her voice threatened to give way to tears. She did feel very grateful; with a reference from Lady Puntney, and perhaps more help from Lady Derwent, she should indeed be able to find a position in another part of the country. She also, however, felt deeply, deeply sad.

Lady Puntney pushed her chair back, stood, walked round the table and held her hands out to Anna. 'Come.' As Anna stood, she pulled her into an embrace.

Anna did not mean to cry—in fact she was very keen *not* to do so—but somehow she found herself weeping onto Lady Puntney's shoulder as the other woman held her.

Eventually, she pulled away, and saw that Lady Puntney's cheeks were also tear-stained.

'I shall miss you greatly,' Lady Puntney said. 'I am angry with the duke and with this situation. I can no longer employ you but please remember that you have a friend in me.'

'Thank you.' Anna was still sniffing a little. She did fully understand Lady Puntney's position. If one were fortunate enough to have a good reputation, one had to guard it fiercely, and Lady Puntney had her three young daughters to think about.

'I cannot bear to think of you cast out entirely,' Lady Puntney told her. 'I am sure I could find somewhere in the country for you to stay, a cottage for you to reside in perhaps. Perhaps you should stay in a hotel while I attempt to organise something for you.'

Anna shook her head. 'Truly, that is most kind, but I can't allow you to do that.'

'You will have to make me a promise. You must not allow yourself to become destitute.'

Anna swallowed as she nodded, all too aware that such a promise might be difficult to keep.

Chapter Fourteen

James

Two days later, James handed his horse's reins to his groom and strode into his house, almost knocking over his butler, Lumley, on his way in.

'Is everything all right, Your Grace?' Lumley asked.

'Yes, thank you,' James lied.

'You seemed to be in a hurry,' Lumley persisted.

It was excellent having household retainers whom one had known one's entire life. Usually. Sometimes, like now, it was not excellent; it was really quite annoying.

'No particular hurry,' James said, and hurried away. Truth be told, he'd been doing everything fast over the past couple of days. This morning, he'd been dressed before his valet had had a chance to get his hands on his wardrobe and he'd practically gobbled his breakfast. He'd galloped hell for leather down Rotten Row. And now he was going to read his correspondence fast before perhaps going and raining blows in Gentleman Jackson's Boxing Saloon.

It was as though he had a compulsion to do things fast and furiously, to try to prevent the thoughts and the misery and the worry that kept intruding.

It wasn't working; as he sat down at his desk, he was, yet again, thinking about Anna. He was angry, although not with her; it was the situation. And himself, of course; he was definitely angry with himself. He was missing her. And he was worried about her; he hoped that she wouldn't be too upset.

He was *really* missing her. He just wanted to see her, talk to her, kiss her—obviously.

God.

Correspondence rushed through, followed by furious sparring with Gentleman Jackson himself, the freneticism of which earnt him some puzzled questioning, and then a gobbled luncheon and some more high-speed work, he found himself sitting with his mother in her boudoir.

He'd been avoiding her for the past two days, sure that she would ask him about Anna, and very eager to avoid talking to her about the situation.

'I am just returned from a call to the Countess of Maltby,' she told him. She looked down at the sewing in her lap for a moment. 'She had much to say on many topics.'

James felt himself tense a little. He did not wish to discuss Anna at all. Thank heavens he had not at any point told his mother that she was the ninth Earl of Broome's granddaughter.

'She asked about you and Miss Blake,' his mother continued, still looking at her embroidery, meaning that he was unable to see the expression in her eyes, 'and I told her, of course, that Miss Blake is an acquaintance of yours and the goddaughter of Lady Derwent, and that I have no further information about her.'

James said nothing.

'I presume that others will also be asking about her. Your attentions to her were most pronounced at the opera, and I hear that you were seen with her more than once at Gunter's.'

This was why he'd been avoiding his mother.

James drew a deep breath. He should say something that would ensure that Miss Blake's reputation would be damaged no further; if there was gossip surrounding her, she might lose her position.

His attentions to her *had* been very pronounced. He should acknowledge that to his mother, and ensure that she believed that Miss Blake had turned him down. Which she had. Except… Had it, in fact, been the case that he had walked away from her once she had told him about her parents? Without trying hard enough to persuade her to accept his proposal?

No, that was something to think about later.

'I was indeed courting Miss Blake,' he said. 'Unfortunately, she does not wish to marry me.'

'What?' His mother dropped her embroidery and her head came straight up. 'Am I to understand that you proposed to her?'

'Yes.'

'You did not tell me of this.'

'I am a grown man, Mama. There are some things that one does not wish to discuss with one's parent or indeed with anyone.'

'You proposed to her and she refused you?'

'That is correct.'

'Why would any young lady in her right mind turn down a proposal from you? You are handsome, you are a wonderful man, and you are a *duke*.'

Because she was a very courteous and considerate young lady. And honest. She could have withheld the information about her parentage until he was too far embroiled in their betrothal to be able to withdraw, had he been so minded.

Why *had* he been so minded when he heard the information?

Oh, yes. The impact that the scandal might have on his mother and sisters.

Miss Blake, though. What if he had compromised her? Well, he had. It was just that no one knew. *He* knew, though.

'James?'

'Sorry, Mama.' He'd been asked why Anna would refuse him. 'I believe that she just did not wish to marry me. She thanked me for my very kind offer and told me that she was very grateful but believed that we should not suit.'

'How could the life of a duchess not suit a *governess*?'

'Perhaps she—' James swallowed '—perhaps Miss Blake wishes to marry for love, as I know you did.'

'Well.' His mother's eyes were practically flashing with anger. 'How could she not love *you*? She could not find a better man.'

'I believe that you are biased, Mama.' James knew that she was wrong. A better man than he would not have allowed things to develop the way they had with

Anna. And, having allowed that to happen, he would have worked out a way to do the right thing for her while avoiding scandal for his family.

'I am not wrong. The young lady is clearly addle-brained.'

'Mama!'

'I make no apology, James. If I cannot state my mind in front of my own son, before whom might I speak frankly?'

James nodded. Fair enough, he supposed.

'I will say that I hope that you are not too distraught. While I am not sure of what family Miss Blake is, she is clearly a lady, and if she would have made you happy, I would have been pleased to welcome her into our family. If she refused you, perhaps she has a reason and perhaps it is for the best. There are many other young ladies who would like to make your acquaintance.'

'Indeed.' James nodded unenthusiastically. Of course there were. He was a duke. Unfortunately for him, he couldn't imagine ever liking—loving—another young lady in the way that he did Anna. And while he had not wanted to marry for love, he also couldn't imagine spending time with another woman, making love to another woman.

'I see that your spirits are currently low.' His mother shook her head. 'I am sorry, James.'

'Thank you, Mama. For your concern. We do not need to speak of it, however.'

'I shall not mention it ever again,' his mother said, almost certainly inaccurately. 'Let me distract you by telling you about some of the other *on-dits* that the countess shared with me.'

'Mama, this is how unpleasant gossip spreads.'

'James. You are my son. Neither of us needs to re-peat any of this further, but one needs to be able to talk to *some*one.'

James immediately felt guilty. He knew how much she missed his father, and his brothers, and of course she needed to be able to talk to him.

And she was right; he needed to be distracted.

'Tell me everything,' he said.

'And *that*,' concluded his mother at least fifteen min-utes later, after she'd regaled him with a series of the most bewilderingly convoluted anecdotes he'd heard in some time, 'goes to show that Miss Blake is indeed an unusual young lady. And while she is of course not of a family of note—' she was entirely wrong there, with re-gard to both the Earl of Broome, and the scandal Anna's parents had caused '—she is very prettily behaved and quite beautiful. And if the Marquis of Blythe can marry an *actress*, you can marry a nonentity.'

'Firstly, Miss Blake does not wish to marry me. And secondly, will the marquis not be subject to approba-tion?' James asked.

'Some perhaps, but it will soon be forgotten if he ig-nores it. He is the Marquis of Blythe, James.'

James stared at his mother. Was she…right? If he were to marry Miss Blake—if she would have him, which he strongly doubted now—would Society effec-tively forgive him? And therefore might there be no neg-ative effect on his mother and sisters?

'There are so many instances of august men marrying women of inferior status,' his mother was continuing. 'If the lady in question is very lady*like*, her supposed unsuitability is easily forgotten as soon as the next little scandal comes along.'

'I had not thought you so pragmatic,' he said. 'When you were compiling a list of prospective brides for me, you were particularly interested in birth.'

'I was. But...' His mother paused and then placed her embroidery on the little side table next to her. 'Come and sit next to me.'

James rose and took his place on the sofa next to her with a level of enthusiasm not much greater than he would have felt had she been a hungry lion.

To his alarm, his mother took his hands in hers.

'I want you to be happy,' she said. 'I know that you did not expect ever to inherit the dukedom and that you now bear a great weight of responsibility that you did not expect.' She hesitated and then squeezed his hands. 'I...saw you with Miss Blake. She is perhaps not of the highest birth, but she is of course vouched for by Sophonora, Lady Derwent. While Sophonora is, as you know, not one of my closest friends, no one can say she is not of the highest *ton*. Anyway, when you were with Miss Blake, you looked...happy, carefree, playful...in *love*.'

James was almost physically squirming by the time she had finished. *Who* had to endure such a conversation with anyone, let alone their own mother? This was even worse than being fussed over by one's housekeeper or butler.

'Sadly,' he said, wondering how soon he could pull his hands out of his mother's clasp, 'as I mentioned, the lady does not wish to marry me.'

'That is a great shame and I think she's very silly and

I am quite angry with her.' His mother still wasn't letting go of his hands.

'No. There is no good reason to be angry with her.' He couldn't believe that he himself had felt anger with her for one second.

If Anna *would* have him, if he told her that he did not care about her birth, would he wish to marry her? He *should* do so, obviously, having compromised her, even if no one had seen them. But would he *wish* to? Given that loving someone deeply carried such a risk of terrible pain if you lost them?

He looked at his mother, who was still holding his hands, and felt a sudden almost overwhelming pang for her loss. And for his own.

'Since we have been speaking plainly,' he said, 'may I ask if you would do it again? Marry my father? Even though you have now lost him?'

His mother stared at him for a long moment, and then said, 'That is a silly question, because I have my children. But even without all of you, certainly I would. I am very lucky to have had the time with your father that I did, and I would have been lucky however long it might have been. I would not have changed anything. James… Are you concerned about loving someone and then losing them?'

'Well, I…' Suddenly he really wished that he could confide in her, talk to her, tell her everything about Anna. But he couldn't, because she had already borne great loss and she already had far too much to worry about. And she was clearly wondering whether the loss of his father and brothers had damaged him in some way. Perhaps it had, but she did not need to know that.

'No,' he said. 'No. The truth about my acquaintance with Miss Blake is that I liked her very tolerably and proposed marriage to her, but she felt that she did not wish to become a duchess with all that that entailed. And that she did not love me quite as she felt she would like to love a husband.' It was a little horrifying how easily the lies rolled off his tongue, but it was necessary, he felt, to protect his mother.

He suddenly felt as though he would like to go for a walk, to clear his head.

'Would you care to accompany me for a walk?' he asked her, out of politeness, because now he really wanted to be alone, to have the time to clarify his thoughts.

'I should have liked that very much, and would like to do so tomorrow, if you have the time, but today I have agreed to shop for a new muff with Sybilla, a most important task, you must recognise.' She twinkled at him and kissed his cheek.

He smiled back at her and stood up. 'I will take my leave of you now, then, and will perhaps see you for dinner later.'

He let himself out of the house shortly afterwards and began to walk aimlessly down the road, as though all his energy had been diverted to his thoughts.

It all suddenly seemed quite simple.

He was a duke. Anna's grandfather was an earl. Her parents had created a scandal. She was, however, indisputably a lady of quality, in her demeanour, her personality, everything. More importantly, she was kind and honourable. She was also very beautiful, and he loved being with her. He loved everything about her in fact.

And one of the advantages of being a duke was, as his mother had said, that his status would transcend a generation-old scandal. And his sisters would have large dowries, which, combined with their birth, should of course allow them to marry whomever they chose.

And, really, that had all been obvious, or should have been, all along.

Had he been using it as an excuse?

Because he had been scared of getting hurt?

He'd behaved appallingly. *Appallingly.*

He had compromised her, whether or not anyone else knew about it—he trusted they did not. He should have proposed to her irrespective of whether or not he *wished* to marry her.

But he *did* wish to marry her, he realised as he rounded another corner and nearly walked into a tree. He wanted to spend as much time with her as he could, make her happy, look after her. If that time was limited, then he would still be lucky to have had that time with her.

But, good God, what if *she* loved *him*—if that were possible after the way he'd behaved—and he died young like his father and brothers had?

According to his mother, being with James would still have been worth it for Anna.

And from a practical perspective, Anna would still, presumably, be much better off as a dowager duchess than as an impecunious governess.

His pace had picked up, he realised, and his steps were leading him in the direction of Bruton Street.

By the time he arrived there, not long afterwards, he was almost running, in a particularly undignified fashion.

Banging on the door knocker, he realised that he must be wearing a very foolish grin at the thought of seeing Anna again.

God, he hoped that he would be able to convince her that she should marry him. If, of course, she did wish to. Perhaps she didn't. Perhaps she didn't love him. Perhaps…

'Good afternoon. I am come to visit Miss Blake,' he said to the butler who had just opened the door.

'Miss Blake no longer works here.' The man's sneer was extraordinary.

James's natural inclination would usually be to give him a severe dressing-down, except now he was more concerned with what had happened to Anna and why the man was speaking in such a derogatory fashion.

'Is Lady Puntney at home?' he asked.

'I will enquire.' And, good God, there was that sneer again. James had rarely ever been spoken to like this and he did not appreciate it. And damn, if the man would speak to *him* like this, how had he spoken to Anna?

As he waited in a very luxuriously decorated drawing room, his level of anxiety about Anna climbed as he had time to wonder further what might have happened to her.

The butler's sneering indicated that she might well have left under some kind of cloud; James very much hoped that that had nothing to do with him but the more he thought about it…

'Good afternoon.' Lady Puntney's smile was pleasant; James was not surprised given what Anna had told him about what a generous employer she had been.

'Good afternoon.' James had no appetite for small talk. 'I came to call on Miss Blake but I understand that she has left your employment. I wondered if you would be able to reassure me that she has come to no ill, and to furnish me with her new direction.'

'I...' Lady Puntney looked over her shoulder, and then took the few steps necessary to reach the door and close it, before moving to a chair near the fireplace. 'Please sit down.'

James inclined his head and took the chair to the other side of the fireplace, and waited, with some impatience.

'I very much like Miss Blake,' Lady Puntney began. 'And I have worried about her since she left.'

'May I ask why she left?'

'She... Well. This is awkward, but I feel that for Miss Blake's sake I should speak plainly. My housekeeper overheard a conversation between the two of you, and one of our housemaids had seen some rather...warm... behaviour between you. I could not, for the sake of my daughters and our reputation as a family, keep Miss Blake on.'

Damn. *Damn.* James had caused Anna so much harm. He wished she had told him what had happened; she could obviously have contacted him. She would not have wished to put him to any trouble, though.

God. He *hated* to think of her enduring the misery of losing her position. And where was she now? What if she had been cast out by all her acquaintance for what was *their* indiscretion, his and hers, not just hers?

'Could I ask where she is now?'

'I'm afraid that I promised her that I would not tell you. I assure you, however, that I understand her to be well and safe for the time being. We have corresponded.'

Lady Puntney was unshakeable in her refusal to betray her promise to Miss Blake, and James left soon afterwards.

He went straight to Lady Derwent's mansion. If anyone knew where Anna was, it must surely be her.

Lady Derwent was not at home.

'Is Miss Blake residing here?' James asked.

'I have not seen her.' The butler *might* be lying. Or he might be telling the truth. He had the art of impassivity very well mastered.

'Do you know when Lady Derwent will return home?'

'I'm afraid not.'

'I will wait,' James said firmly, and sat himself down on an intricately carved oak chair in the hall, so that no one might enter the house without him seeing.

The chair was hard, the afternoon was long, and James did not enjoy his thoughts; he was very worried about Anna, he felt incredibly guilty, and he was essentially just desperate to see her. It didn't bear thinking about where she might be if she wasn't with her godmother. Except he did think about it.

When, eventually, Lady Derwent did return, James was extremely disappointed to see that she was alone; he had been hoping that Anna might perhaps be with her.

'Your Grace,' she said. 'Interesting.' She handed her gloves to her butler. 'Come into my saloon.'

'What a pleasure it is seeing you,' she said, unsmilingly, as she settled herself on a sofa. 'Please do sit down.'

'Thank you.' James eyed her. He suspected that he would fare a lot better with her if he made the effort to engage in some social niceties, however much he wished—frankly—to yell *Where is my Anna?* 'I hope that you are well?'

'Very well, I thank you. A little frustrated, I must admit.'

'Frustrated?' James felt as though he was at the beginning of an intricate chess game, to which he did not fully know the rules.

'Frustrated,' she confirmed, before lapsing into what he knew was an uncharacteristic silence, and which he felt was perhaps designed to induce him to speak.

He had nothing to lose, he decided, in indulging her, as long as he was cautious.

'I am sorry to hear of your frustration. I myself am also a little frustrated.'

Lady Derwent raised an eyebrow.

James decided to plunge straight in.

'I love your goddaughter, Miss Blake,' he stated. 'I understand from Lady Puntney that she terminated her employment because of our friendship. Most immediately, I am concerned about her, and hope that she is well and in a place of safety. I would also like very much to speak to her, to explain that I was stupid and how much I love her.'

Lady Derwent nodded, thoughtfully. 'I see.' She looked as though she was thinking very hard.

'I would, therefore, be very grateful if you were able to tell me where she is.'

'I am able,' she said, speaking slowly, 'to tell you that she is safe and well and that I have seen her. And that I will do my utmost to ensure that she remains safe and well.'

'Thank God,' James said.

'Yes.'

James looked at her, looking at him, as though she was sizing him up, and waited. He had already asked if she knew where Anna was, and he didn't think she was a lady who would appreciate repetition.

'I understand that you and my goddaughter visited Gunter's together twice, in addition to our evening at the opera. My observation was that you had seemed to have become quite close.'

'Yes. I love her,' James repeated.

'And?'

'And I would like to marry her.' He supposed that this was the equivalent of asking a young lady's father if he might be permitted to propose to his daughter. It was not very enjoyable; Lady Derwent's eagle eye was making him squirm as though he were a child, and there was something quite peculiar about declaring his love for Anna to someone other than her. Had he, in fact, told her properly how very much he loved her? He wasn't sure that he had.

He cleared his throat. 'And therefore I would very much welcome the opportunity to see her again. I wondered if you knew where she was.'

'My goddaughter was very distressed, although doing her best to hide it, when I saw her. She asked me to promise that I would not tell you whither she fled.'

James nodded. Damn.

'I cannot break my promise to her,' Lady Derwent said. 'She needs to be able to trust *someone*.' A low blow, but fair enough. James should have been thinking more clearly and should not have let things happen the way they had.

'I would like to be able to prove to her that she can trust me,' he said. 'Because, as I mentioned, I would like to marry her, because I love her and would like to do my best to make her happy.'

'Prettily spoken,' Lady Derwent finally approved. 'I would like you to be able to propose to her again, *properly*, but I cannot break my promise. Perhaps… Let me think.'

And then she sat and thought, while James fought very hard not to tap his fingers or his foot or just say—shout—*Yes, what?*

Eventually, she said, 'I will send you a note later.'

That was it? She was going to send him a note? What if she didn't send it?

He looked at her. Yes, this was, unfortunately, clearly the most she was going to give him.

'Thank you,' he said, managing not to grit his teeth too much, and rose to leave.

Lady Derwent's note arrived in Berkeley Square shortly after he did.

Pulling it out of its envelope with fingers that were suddenly all thumbs, he discovered that Lady Derwent had merely written:

I will be at Hatchard's bookshop at eleven o'clock tomorrow morning and should like to meet you there.

The frustration was immense. Maybe he should try to ask Lady Maria Swanley if she knew where her friend was now. He half turned back towards the front door, before checking himself. He should not cause any more gossip than had already arisen. He would have to wait, and hope that Lady Derwent had something more interesting to tell him on the morrow than she had today.

He was at Hatchard's the next morning ten minutes before the hour, wishing to make very sure that he did not miss Lady Derwent.

The last time he had visited this shop had been to purchase books for Anna.

Really, everywhere and everything reminded him of her.

Dear *God*, he missed her.

Her humour.

Her quick understanding.

Her smile.

The way she made him feel when he was with her… complete, happy, as though there was nowhere he'd rather be.

He hoped so very desperately that she was all right.

As he stood there, thinking and worrying about Anna, he realised that he was beginning to *see* her everywhere, imagine that she was in front of him.

At this rate he would be accosting complete strangers thinking that they were her.

For example, at this moment he could see a smallish woman making her way along the road towards him, and for some reason—probably the way she moved—she reminded him so strongly of Anna that he could almost believe that she *was* Anna.

So much so, in fact, that it was difficult not to stare at her.

Especially since, as she drew closer, he could see that her hair was of the same colour and…

And… He blinked hard. It *was* her.

It was Anna.

Walking down Piccadilly towards him.

Chapter Fifteen

⟡

Anna

Anna had not particularly wished to visit Hatchard's—or anywhere else—this morning, but she was deeply beholden to her godmother, and it did do her good to leave the house and take some walks, rather than moping inside, wondering what was to become of her, so she had agreed to join her when she had suggested this excursion.

The proposed outing had been for them to visit the shops together, but at the last moment Lady Derwent had told Anna that she was a little fatigued and thought that she would do well to rest this morning as she had a busy day ahead of her, but that she most particularly wanted to purchase Jane Austen's *Northanger Abbey*, and she would be very grateful if Anna would go on her behalf to buy it.

Anna had vaguely wondered that her godmother wouldn't send a footman in her stead, but perhaps Lady Derwent was trying to ensure that Anna was kept occupied. She was clearly right to do so, because it had certainly not been making Anna happy sitting inside reflecting on the turn that her fortunes had taken and what might have been.

She would also, of course, be able to browse the bookshelves herself, which she would enjoy. Reading was always helpful in taking one away from one's own problems.

As long as one could concentrate and a large duke did not intrude too much into one's thoughts.

She looked along the road at the shop as she approached and...

Discovered that the duke was yet again intruding into her thoughts.

Because, being fanciful, she could easily imagine that the large man standing outside the building was him.

Oh...*was* she imagining it, or was it actually him?

It couldn't be.

But that height and those broad shoulders, topped by his handsome face and thick, dark hair.

It...*was* him.

It was definitely him.

He was his usual elegant self, attired in a plain but perfectly cut dark coat, *very* attractively fitting breeches— *why* was her stupid brain thinking about *that* at this moment?—and impressively shiny boots.

His expression and posture were not as usual, though. He was entirely still, almost frozen, his hands fixed to his stick, his eyes staring and his jaw a little dropped.

If she hadn't been so stunned, she might almost have laughed at the way in which he was the personification of astonishment; it seemed that he had expected to see her as little as she had expected to see him.

For a long moment, Anna felt very much as though she imagined a chicken might in the presence of an unexpected fox—panic-stricken and unable to think—before she gathered her wits and wondered whether she might be able to just keep on walking, into the shop, and pretend she had never seen him. Apart from the stomach churning and near-faintness she was feeling, of course, but if she could just sit down for a moment, she was sure she would recover quite quickly.

Or perhaps she would just turn about and go somewhere else for a while and return when she was sure he would have left.

But, 'Good morning,' he said, while she was still trying to work out what she should do.

Oh.

'Good morning.' Her voice sounded distinctly odd.

'Good morning,' he repeated, before shaking his head. 'Apparently my wits are addled; that is the second *good morning* I have offered you.' His rueful smile was *so* attractive.

Anna found her own lips curling into a little smile too, which was odd, because she was fairly sure that she was still angry with him. She would not show it, however; she would rather retain any scrap of dignity she might have.

'Well, thank you for those good mornings.' She pointed at the clouds above them. 'They are not particularly apt.' Conversing about the weather was always a good ploy when there were no other topics that one wished to discuss. A few more weather-related words and she would be able to go inside and try to forget that she had seen him.

'Oh, no, they are extremely apt. Seeing you makes this morning good.'

'Oh!' Really? He sounded as though he was flirting with her. Was that usual behaviour in this situation? Surely not.

She should go; she really did not want to talk to him. Well, if she was honest, she *did* wish to talk to him, but it could only lead to further misery.

'It was most enjoyable to see you but I'm afraid I am rather busy.' She began to move past him towards the shop entrance.

'I had expected to see Lady Derwent here,' he said, just as she drew level with him. 'She asked me to meet her here. Is she joining you?'

Anna slowed to a halt. 'I... Oh. No, she isn't. She is unfortunately a little tired this morning, so she asked me to come and purchase some books for her.' She frowned. 'When did she ask you to meet you here?'

'I received a note from her yesterday evening instructing me to meet her here at eleven o'clock this morning.' He looked at his watch. 'Exactly now, in fact.'

Anna frowned. 'She is not forgetful,' she said slowly.

'Indeed,' the duke agreed. 'She could not possibly have forgotten that she had arranged to meet me here...'

'...when she requested me to join her on an excursion here, and then at the very last moment said that she was too tired to come but urged me to leave immediately because it looked as though it was going to rain,' Anna finished.

She shook her head.

Her godmother had *promised* her that she would not

tell anyone—especially the duke—that she was stay-ing with her.

She had not told him, it seemed. She had planned this meeting instead. Why, though? What purpose could it serve?

None. No purpose. And, for goodness' sake, now her eyes were filling yet again.

'I think we both know,' she said with an effort, 'that there can be no benefit in our conversing. I will bid you goodbye.' She stepped towards the shop door.

'Lady Derwent had good reason to decide to orches-trate our meeting,' the duke said.

Anna stopped again and turned to look at him.

'I visited her yesterday afternoon,' he continued. 'Do I understand that you are staying with her? She did not tell me that.'

'Yes, I am; I asked her to tell no one.'

He nodded. 'It seems that she wished us to meet but did not wish to betray your confidence.'

'Yes.' Anna knew that she shouldn't ask, but she couldn't help it: 'May I ask why you visited her?'

'Because I wanted to tell you...' The duke looked around. 'This is really not the place for it. Would you care to walk with me?'

Anna was so very tempted. But she had been tempted by him before now, and it had cost her dearly. Now, on the off chance that she still had any reputation left, she must guard it carefully, and could not be seen with any men, especially the duke.

'No, thank you.' She took another step towards the door. 'I am going to do the errand I came to do for my godmother and then I am going to leave.'

'You know, I think I also have a fancy to purchase some books.'

'That was really not what I intended,' Anna told him. A little weakly, because, if she was honest, she didn't entirely want him to leave.

'I think it might have been what your godmother intended.'

'My godmother is wonderful but she is not always right. As we have already ascertained.'

She was very frequently right, though.

The duke pushed the door open and smiled at her.

Anna rolled her eyes at him and then stepped inside. He had a look in his eye that told her that he was about to say something quite outrageous. He would not be *able* to be truly outrageous inside the shop, though; they would run the risk of being overheard, and, while she didn't think he was easily embarrassed on his own account, she did think that he was likely not to wish to embarrass *her*. So there couldn't *really* be any danger in talking to him. Just a little.

When she got inside, she realised that this place was quite heavenly. She would have to return, if she was able, another time, when she wouldn't be distracted by the duke's presence.

'Is this the first time you have been here?' he asked as she looked around. Gazing at the shelves and shelves of books was infinitely easier than looking at him and reflecting on the miserable fact that their lives would diverge again after this ridiculous meeting.

'Yes.'

'It is quite special, is it not? Even I—not, as you know, a great book-lover—can sense magic here.'

'Yes.'

'What books are you here to purchase?' the duke pursued.

'I have a list from my godmother and she suggested that I also buy one or two of my choice, which is of course very kind in her.'

'What books are you thinking of purchasing for yourself?'

'I don't know. I'm afraid that I will need to take some time choosing them. Probably in silence.' She didn't want to sound as though she was encouraging him to talk to her.

She took a few steps further into the shop.

The duke followed her.

Several pairs of eyes rose from books and shelves to look at them.

'I wonder whether you should leave me now,' she whispered. 'We have been remarked. I do not wish to be the subject of any further gossip.'

'Of course,' he replied, also whispering. 'And of course I do not wish to force my presence on you, and indeed should probably not have followed you in here, so, if you would like me to leave immediately, I will do so. But before I go could I possibly explain that I have something of great importance to say to you?'

'I think we have already discussed everything there is to say.' Sad but true.

He leaned closer to her and, still whispering, said into her ear, 'I love you.'

Anna froze.

'What?' she said, quite loudly.

'Shhh,' several voices said.

'I love you,' he whisper-repeated.

Anna ignored him and marched down an aisle between two sets of shelves. She was suddenly almost *throbbing* with annoyance. Why had he said that? Why was he torturing her like this? Why was he still following her?

'Please leave,' she hissed over her shoulder.

'Please marry me,' he whispered back.

Anna stopped stock still, and he bumped into her back, nearly sending her flying.

He caught her with a hand on each of her upper arms as she stumbled.

When she was steady, she turned round to face him, filled all of a sudden with heat—*furious* heat—from head to toe.

'We—' she prodded him in the chest with her finger '—have already discussed this. The answer, if you remember, was no.'

'You told me that the reason was that your parents had caused a scandal.'

'Shhh,' someone said.

'My apologies,' the duke said.

'I don't care about scandal,' he whispered. 'The only reason I cared about it was that I was worried about my sisters. But that is ridiculous. I love you more than words could ever say and, if you love me too, I would like to spend the rest of our days together doing my best to make you as happy as possible.'

'No,' Anna stated.

'No what?'

'No, I will not marry you.'

'You should marry him,' a woman said from the other side of the shelves.

'Hmmmph,' Anna told her.

'Would you like to go outside to discuss this better?' the duke whispered. 'I had not planned to propose here in such a manner.'

'I am so sorry that your proposal is ruined—' Anna hoped that her words sounded as insincere as they were '—but I'm afraid that I do not wish to go outside with you.'

'Oh, please *do* go,' the woman from the other side of the shelves begged.

James mouthed, 'Please?' at her.

'Well...'

'Only if you don't mind,' he suddenly said. 'I do not wish to pressure you into doing anything you do not wish to do.'

'Indeed,' replied Anna, even as the treacherous part of her brain reflected that however annoying and infuriating James might be, he could not help himself also being remarkably kind and chivalrous; it did not occur to a great number of men to allow women the courtesy of making decisions, big or small, about their own lives.

'Good day to you,' she told him, conscious of a great weight of misery descending as she uttered the words.

Her misery was reflected in his face, she saw, as he opened his mouth to reply.

She didn't hear what he had to say, because they were interrupted by a woman sweeping into the end of their aisle.

'Amscott!' she said.

'Lady Fortescue.' He bowed his head slightly.

'I am the lady with whom you were communicating through the shelves,' she said. She turned her gimlet gaze on Anna and said, 'I do not know who you are, and do not think that now is the time for introductions. I am come to say that I think that you really ought to hear him out, in a better location than here. Now that I see who it is who loves you and wishes to marry you, I have to tell you that you are quite mad if you do not accept him, although that is of course entirely your own business.'

A *shhh* came from behind the shelves opposite where Lady Fortescue had been.

'Quite.' She made a shooing motion with her hands. 'Off you go.'

'I should very much like the opportunity to have private conversation with you.' James was not moving, the shooing apparently having no effect on him. 'But I do understand if you wish not to.'

As a matter of principle, Anna did not wish to speak further to him. But, also, she very much did.

It would be silly to allow her principles to cause her to wonder for ever what he might have said.

And she had already been very miserable because of him; it could hardly make matters worse.

'Perhaps a very short conversation,' she said.

'Very sensible,' Lady Fortescue approved. 'Please go now and leave the rest of us in peace. I shall of course say nothing about this to anyone should it come to nothing. If it *does* come to something, I shall expect to be a guest of honour at your wedding.'

Despite everything, Anna felt her lips twitch a little. She wondered if her godmother and Lady Fortescue knew each other well. They would certainly be a match for each other in the forcefulness stakes.

'I will bear that in mind.' James indicated behind him with his eyes and Anna nodded. 'Good day, my lady.'

And then they traipsed out of the shop, regarded the entire way—Anna could feel her eyes boring into her back—by Lady Fortescue.

When they got outside, they discovered that it was raining.

'Oh, dear.' James looked down at her with a rueful smile. 'I must hope that the weather is not indicative of the outcome of our conversation. Let us find a hackney. If you would like?'

'I would prefer to walk.' Anna tried not to be conscious of the damp already working its way inside the neckline of her pelisse. 'Your reputation is already going to be quite ruined by Lady Fortescue having overheard our conversation. If we enter a carriage together it will be even worse. And I myself must be very careful.'

'I do not care about my own reputation but fully understand your point about your own. I apologise. Let us walk instead, if you would like?'

'Thank you.'

As they began to stroll up Piccadilly, James said, 'Your comment about my reputation leads me directly to one of the things I was going to mention to you. If you are happy to hear what I have to say?'

'I am not sure that *happy* is the word,' Anna said cautiously.

'But?'

'But if you wish to say something to me, please do.'

If she was honest, she was quite desperate to hear what he had to say.

It began to rain significantly harder.

'Should we perhaps stand over here?' James led her in the direction of some large trees. The rain was so hard that Anna could ascertain no more than that they had very broad trunks.

It was a little less wet under the trees, but by no means dry.

'A good thing about it being so rainy is that we are unlikely to be remarked by anyone at all.' Anna was damp all over now. This was the kind of weather that caused less robust persons to become quite ill; and she had a nasty feeling that it would take her several hours to feel completely dry again.

'That is very true. A good thing.' James cleared his throat. 'Thank you for agreeing to listen to what I have to say. I don't think now is the time for small talk. Both because of the rain and because, well, because of what has already passed between us.'

'I agree.' Anna slightly wanted to stamp her foot. 'So what is it that you wish to say?'

'You are right; I was in fact engaging in small talk.'

'As you still are…'

He laughed. 'Sorry. Yes. Right. Well.'

Anna finally lost the ability to be at all patient. 'Oh. My. Goodness,' she said.

'Yes. Of course. Well. I have one big message for you.'

'What is that message?' Anna asked.

'I love you and would be the happiest man alive if you would agree to marry me, and I have several smaller messages which combine to create that one. Are you happy for me to continue?'

'Yes I am and thank you for asking.' Really, she didn't feel at all thankful; she just wanted him to *get on with it.*

'I spend a lot of time with sycophants, who will listen to anything I say merely because I am a duke,' he surprised her by replying, 'and I have no desire to force my conversation on you. Although I *am* extremely pleased that you are happy to listen.'

Anna nodded, just about managing not to roll her eyes. Had anyone, ever, in the history of irritating conversations, been as slow to say whatever it was they had to say?

'So,' he said. 'I didn't know that I would see you this morning. I feel as though I should really have prepared a speech. As I did not, I must apologise if my train of thought is a little rambling.'

Anna could contain herself no longer. 'It is extremely rambling,' she told him.

James nodded and smiled ruefully. 'I'm sorry. I feel as though this is the most important conversation of my life and as though I must not get it wrong.'

Anna just raised her eyebrows.

He laughed, before looking serious again.

'Here I go, then,' he said. 'You referred to my reputation. As I mentioned just now, I am surrounded by sycophants. That is because of my rank and my wealth. And as mentioned by mother recently, if I marry someone whose parents acted in a scandalous fashion a generation ago, no one would dare to mention it to me, and it would not have any impact on my mother and sisters, about whose reputations I of course care deeply. It would also not have any impact on my wife because I would not permit that to happen.' He looked suddenly very haughty and very ducal.

'I'm not sure...' she began to reply.

'Not sure?'

'I don't know.' If it was genuinely the case that the scandal would not ruin him—or his family—should she, could she marry him?

She didn't know. He had walked away from her very fast after his proposal the night of the opera. Why hadn't he tried to convince her immediately that they should marry? Would he be just like her grandfather and her father and not remain steadfast in the face of difficulty, or when he perhaps grew bored with her?

He cut across her thoughts. 'I'm not sure that that was the first thing that I should have mentioned. In fact, on reflection, I know that of course it isn't. I wish I had prepared what I was going to say.' He drew a deep breath. 'What I should have told you just now—and what I should have told you when I asked you to marry me— is that I am scared.'

'Scared?' Anna frowned, confused.

As she looked up at him, she saw him swallow and press his lips together, and suddenly she just wanted to put her arms around him, pull him against her, and pro- vide reassurance against whatever was worrying him. Of course, on the face of it she had a lot more to be scared about than she did—for all she knew she could easily end up in the workhouse after all—but huge privilege did not preclude someone from feeling fear, and he had of course lost several close relatives quite recently. Per- haps it was related to that.

'I have been scared about many things. My father died quite young and my brothers very young, as you know. I found the pain of losing them very hard, both on my own account and that of my mother and sisters. I do not wish to experience such pain again, and I also do not wish to be the cause of someone else experiencing such pain. It seems to me that loving someone is therefore dangerous.'

Anna nodded slowly.

'With regard to loving you, I now realise that living without you, missing you, worrying about you, will cause me huge pain. And so, selfishly, I would like to marry you. I am worried, though, that I will die young as my male relatives did, and leave you to experience pain. I believe, however, that what I have to offer you is—baldly speaking—more than just myself as a husband; if something *were* to happen to me, you would be the Dowager Duchess of Amscott and—if we were lucky—the mother of the next duke, and your future would be secure.'

'Is that your reason for proposing?' she asked. 'Pity? Charity? To secure my future now that you know that my employment was terminated?'

'No. *No.* Of course not.' He sounded almost impatient. 'I could settle a large sum of money on you. I could employ you myself. I could buy you a house. Anonymously so that no scandal would attach to the purchase. I could do any manner of things to secure your future. And if you do not wish to marry me I will of course accept that, and I will beg you to allow me to help you financially. But securing your future *would* be a happy side effect of your marrying me.'

'Oh.'

It was a lot to comprehend.

After a few moments of reflection, she said, 'I am scared too.'

James nodded, his eyes fixed on her face, but did not speak.

'I'm scared of losing someone, as you are, but I think perhaps we all are, and something I have learnt is that it is wise to take happiness wherever one finds it.'

'I agree that that is wise.' He had his hands clasped in front of him, so hard that the knuckles were whitening, and his gaze was very intent.

'However,' she continued, 'I am also scared of relinquishing my independence to any man. My grandfather disowned my mother. My father abandoned us both.'

James swallowed visibly and said, 'I can understand that. I can offer you every assurance that your heart and your security would be safe with me, but I don't know how to convince you of that. Maybe... I can't. I love you, though. I would never...' His voice sounded harsh, raw.

Anna just stared at him, mute.

'I...' He stopped, swallowed again, and then continued, 'I believe that my happiness is bound up in you. I would very much like to marry you. I love you. I love your smile. I love your laugh. I love the way you make *me* laugh so much. I love your kindness. I love the way you tilt your head to one side and press your lips together when you are particularly annoyed and clearly fighting with yourself not to give someone—me—a stern set-down.'

Anna laughed, and then sniffed.

'I love everything I know of you,' James continued,

'and I would count myself indescribably fortunate to have the opportunity to spend a lifetime learning as much about you as I may. I would never disown you or abandon you.'

Anna sniffed tears back, suddenly—she could not say why—sure that he was not like her grandfather or father.

Of *course* not all men were the same. Take the Puntneys. Sir Laurence was clearly a most devoted husband. And Lady Maria's parents were happily married. Perhaps Anna had just been unlucky with her grandfather and father.

Perhaps her luck had turned when she met the duke.

'Oh,' she said.

'I would like so very much to marry you. And love and protect you for ever. I have never been surer about anything in my life.'

Anna sniffed and smiled at the same time.

For the first time since they'd moved under the tree, James began to smile too.

He unclasped his hands and reached for hers, before pulling her gently so that they were standing quite close together.

Then he got down on one knee, on the very wet ground, in full view of anyone who might walk past, and said, 'Anna Blake. I love you more than I can describe. Would you do me the great honour of accepting my hand in marriage?'

His features—so harshly handsome in repose, so delightful when laughing, but always giving the impression of strength, were arranged now in what Anna could only think of as vulnerable hope. It was the most beautiful expression she'd ever seen anyone wear.

'I love your face,' she whispered.

James screwed his loveable face up a little and then raised his eyebrows.

'And I also love *you*,' she told him.

James was still kneeling, still holding her hands.

'I cannot imagine anything better than being able to spend every day at your side,' she said.

'And without wishing to sound too impatient...?'

'I would love to marry you.'

'Oh, my God. Thank you.' He kissed each of her hands in turn, before rising to his feet—a most delightful flexing of his thigh muscles visible through his breeches as he did so—and drawing her into his arms. 'I love you more than words can say.'

And then he kissed her extremely thoroughly and extremely scandalously right there on the pavement, under the trees, in the rain, and it was quite wonderful.

Epilogue

Anna

The Lake District,
Christmas 1827

Anna tilted her head to one side as she regarded herself in the floor-length looking glass in front of her.

James appeared behind her. 'You look beautiful, as always.' He slid his arms around her waist and kissed the top of her head.

Anna allowed herself a moment to enjoy the pleasurable shiver his touch always gave her, before putting her hands over his and saying, 'We must hurry.'

'Really?' He turned her in his arms so that she was facing him, put one finger under her chin so that her face was raised to his, and kissed her full on the lips.

And then he kissed her again, hungrily, as though he *needed* her, now, even though they had been together only last night and after their ball tonight would be able to fall into bed together again.

Anna *knew* that they should go down to greet their guests, but she couldn't help herself reaching her arms round James's neck, anchoring him to her as their kiss deepened.

Still kissing her, teasing her tongue with his, he suddenly lifted her and carried her the few paces to the bed in the middle of the room and sat down on it with her on his knees.

As his mouth traced kisses into the sensitive skin at the base of her neck, he murmured, 'I very much like this costume.' And then he did something very clever with his fingers, so that suddenly the bodice of it was loosened. With one hand he cupped her breast and with the other he lifted her skirts, and Anna found herself wriggling so that she could move against his hardness.

'I like your costume too,' she panted, as he lifted his pharaoh tunic.

'You make,' James said between groans, as he moved inside her a few minutes later, 'the most alluring Cleopatra.'

'Thank you,' Anna managed to say. 'Oh, *James.*'

Afterwards, he held her close in his arms, until they were both calm.

And then Anna sat up and said, 'James! Our guests are probably already here.'

James moved so that he was lying on his back, looking at her, his hands behind his head.

'If you aren't careful,' he said, 'there will be no possibility of my going downstairs for a *long* time. You look extremely debauched, my beautiful duchess.'

Anna looked down at herself, entirely naked, save for her Cleopatra robe around her waist.

'Honestly,' she tutted. 'We have *guests* downstairs. Many dozens of them.'

It was the tenth anniversary of their wedding and James had arranged for them to visit the Lake District with their children—a long-held desire of Anna's but one that she had been unable to fulfil until now due to regular pregnancies—and spend the Christmas period there in a house on one of his estates. They had invited a large number of house guests, including, naturally, Lady Derwent, Lady Maria and her husband, Clarence—now a vicar with a sizeable parish—and their three children, and the Puntneys, with whom they had become firm friends, and this evening were holding a Christmas ball.

'Lady Derwent will be more than happy to greet them in our absence.'

'That is true but we really should go.' Anna hopped off the bed before James could tempt her to engage in any further lovemaking, and began to re-dress herself.

'I am the luckiest man in the world,' James said, sitting up. 'I have the most wonderful wife a man could ever wish for and five perfect children.' They had four boys and a baby girl, all of whom they doted on most unfashionably.

'And I the luckiest woman.' Anna never referred to the fact out loud, because she did not wish to remind James of past tragedies, but he had now lived several years longer than both his brothers, and appeared in excellent health. And he was the best husband a woman could ever wish for, having proved time and time again to her by his actions and words that he was entirely trustworthy, a very different kind of man from her grandfather and father. Not to mention, of course, very good company and extremely handsome.

They shared one more lingering kiss on the lips before Anna pushed James firmly away, patted her hair back into place and declared herself ready to descend to their party.

As they made their way down the house's grand staircase, they were greeted by a clamour of voices and an almost bewildering array of brightly coloured costumes. They had chosen a masquerade as a nod to Anna's impersonation of Lady Maria on their first meeting at James's mother's ball.

Anna put her mask on and said, 'We should have hidden our costumes from each other to see if we could find each other.'

'There would have been no point. From the very first moment I met you, it was as though I recognised you, even though I did not know your real identity. I would know you anywhere, whatever your disguise.'

'And I you.'

They smiled at each other, before Lady Derwent and James's mother came towards them. The two ladies had buried their differences and were now—usually—on the best of terms.

Except…oh, dear.

Anna glanced at James and saw that he was as wide-eyed as she felt she must be.

'You…both…look magnificent,' he told the two ladies, the merest tremor of laughter in his voice.

'Thank you,' they replied in tandem, neither of them smiling.

Anna decided to address the situation directly.

'I think that you both look truly spectacular and that, since Queen Elizabeth is widely regarded as having been the best of queens, and you are both the best of ladies, it is only right that you should both be her this evening. One can never have too many Queen Elizabeths.'

'Were that true,' Lady Derwent said, 'it would be a very fortunate thing.' She indicated behind her to the room.

And, oh, dear, again. There were a *lot* of Queen Elizabeths.

'I flatter myself that I am wearing better jewels,' Lady Derwent whispered, far too loudly, to Anna.

'I flatter *my*self that I have a smaller waist,' James's mother told James, not bothering to whisper.

James laughed out loud while Anna took an arm of each of the other ladies and said, 'Let us go and seek some refreshment and then perhaps sit down for a moment before the dancing begins.'

They were joined shortly afterwards by Lady Maria. Who was also dressed as Queen Elizabeth.

None of the Queen Elizabeths looked remotely amused.

Anna clapped her hands loudly in panic. 'I think it is time for the dancing to begin.'

Three hours later, she had danced until her feet were sore, including, extremely unfashionably, *three times* with her own husband (he had speculated that no one would know because they were in costume, and Anna had pointed out that everyone would know because there was no other man in the room with the same thick head of hair—greying most attractively now—and broad shoulders), and eaten supper with the openly warring Queen Elizabeths, and she was now taking a little rest, when the most handsome pharaoh in the room approached her.

He bowed low. 'Cleopatra. Would you do me the honour of taking a walk outside with me?'

'I should be delighted.' Truly, she was incredibly blessed that just the sound of her husband's voice could still send a shiver through her after ten years together.

She was shivering in a different way within seconds of going through the doors at the end of the ballroom, onto the terrace that ran along the back of the house above lawns that led down to a lake and beyond that a wood, the whole illuminated now by the full moon in the most fairy-tale-like way.

'It's *freezing*,' she squeaked.

'Indeed it is.' James put his arm round her and hugged her into him. 'This is the only way I can think of to warm you given that I have no coat or jacket to give to you.'

'Mmm, that is nice, but it's still *very* cold.'

'It is indeed too cold to be outside without very warm outer garments,' he agreed. 'I wonder… Perhaps we could sneak around the outside of the house and enter by a side door and make our way up to our chamber without anyone noticing…'

'That is a very good idea,' Anna approved.

And ten minutes later, they tiptoed into their bedchamber, both of them almost snorting with the laughter they were trying to hold back.

And then, almost before the door was closed behind them, James had Anna in his arms.

'You know that I thought about marriage from the very first moment I met you,' he told her between kisses. 'And that I loved you infinitely almost immediately, and yet I love you more with every day that passes. How is that possible?'

'It is the same for me,' Anna told him, as he began to make her gasp with pleasure. 'Thank you for being my wonderful husband. I love you.'

'I love you too.'

And then they spent the night celebrating their first decade of marriage in the most delightful way.

* * * * *

If you loved this story, you'll be sure to love Sophia Williams's other captivating reads:

How the Duke Met His Match
The Secret She Kept from the Earl

Look out for more stories from Sophia Williams, coming soon!

HARLEQUIN
Reader Service

Enjoyed your book?

Try the perfect subscription for Romance readers and get more great books like this delivered right to your door.

See why over 10+ million readers have tried Harlequin Reader Service.

Start with a Free Welcome Collection with free books and a gift—valued over $20.

Choose any series in print or ebook. See website for details and order today:

TryReaderService.com/subscriptions